Praise fo

Lottie
CARDEW

Midsummer
Magic at
Midwynter
Hall

Cloverdilli House
Press

Also by Lottie Cardew

Although this particular book is more of a standalone
compared to the others (it can easily be read out of order)
the chronology of the Pebblestow series to date is
as follows:

A Christmas Wish on a Carousel
One Last Dream for December
Midsummer Magic at Midwynter Hall

An Important Note from the Author
If you are aware of any sensitive topics or triggers that
may adversely affect your experience or enjoyment of a
book, you may wish to refer to the guidance on
my website:

https://bit.ly/LottieCardewContentGuidance

Please note, though, that my stories focus very much on the light, and the many positive aspects of what it means to be human. My books could potentially tug at your heartstrings, but they're ultimately uplifting and brimming with hope. It gives me great pleasure to write them and my wish is for my words to pass this happiness on to you. There's a certain magic when that happens, and I'm perpetually grateful to be able to wield it.

Lottie xx

Paperback edition first published by

© Cloverdilli House Press 2023

ISBN: 978-1-7397758-2-7

Midsummer Magic at Midwynter Hall
Copyright © Lottie Cardew 2023

Cover by Cloverdilli House Graphic Design.

Pamela Ann Hughes

1942 − 2022

For my lovely late mother-in-law and super-fan.
Dearly missed.
If I had the chance to say one last thing, it would be
thank you for raising such an incredible son. He's a
credit to you, and I'll keep taking good care of him
(though he does a better job of taking care of *me*).

xxxxx

'Ah! my dear, I wish you would not make matches and foretell things, for whatever you say always comes to pass.'

JANE AUSTEN, Emma

Chapter 1

'I told you, didn't I?' Perched on the largest of the wicker sofas in the conservatory, I regarded my friend with triumph, anticipating the validation I deserved. 'I always said they were made for each other.'

'Hmm.' Irritatingly, Polly just carried on scrolling. 'I guess.'

'I did!' I said, more emphatically. 'And why can't I just see all the pictures?' It was tantalising to have nothing but a brief glimpse whenever she decided to jiggle her phone in front of my face.

'Because I took a billion, and I'm still trying to decide which to post. Ninety percent of them are just cringe.'

Frustrated, I put out my hand in a grabbing motion, but still she hesitated.

'*Please*, Poll. We established ages ago that your idea of cringe isn't the same as mine, remember?'

With a sigh of defeat, she passed me her phone. 'Just scroll from there, but don't say I didn't warn you.'

'Oh!' I couldn't help exclaiming, with a disturbing jolt of envy. I blinked at one image after another. 'She looks so pretty. That's a gorgeous dress, the sort I like. Elegant and understated, but a bit cottagecore, too. I love that she had flowers in her hair, not a veil or tiara. And it's amazing how you've captured all the blossom flying around. Nature's own confetti.'

'She looked stunning. I knew she would. As for the groom…' Polly's already pink cheeks turned rosier.

I nodded in understanding. I wasn't indifferent to his looks, either, although I'd never met him in person. Or the bride, come to that. But Polly kept her social media regularly updated, and thrived on documenting her life in the village of Pebblestow in vivid detail. It was the only way I could know who these people were. Not just the newlyweds, but the small number of guests in attendance.

Although Polly never posted anyone's picture online without permission, she had a way of taking selfies for her own private albums that "accidentally" featured select people in the background, and through these discreet pictures she dramatised the daily ups and downs of semi-rural life in a soap opera style fashion for my benefit.

My home – Midwynter Hall – lay in a large leafy valley between three villages; Pebblestow being the nearest, and feted for being the prettiest, too. And thanks to my friend,

I had a steady source of local entertainment to tap into.

Watching TV wasn't as personal or immediate as Polly's tales. Many programmes I liked were about far-flung places and dependent on high ratings or racking up five-star reviews. The studio execs wouldn't care whether Emmeline Midwynter over in Shropshire, England, was invested in the story. If the audience figures were low and it was too eye-wateringly expensive to produce, it would be axed.

I hadn't given this much thought, in effect. For the last two years, as long as Polly had been coming to the Hall, I'd accepted and cherished this ray of sunshine in my life. She would never leave me on a cliffhanger if she could help it – she understood what it all meant to me. But as part of the diary assignment I would be working on over the coming weeks, I had to examine if this was a good thing. I wasn't altogether sure why.

It had been proposed to me, one-to-one, by my tutor following a recent group Zoom meeting, after the other students had vanished from my screen, as if they'd abruptly ceased to exist (until the class WhatsApp group would point to the contrary).

'Are Polly's visits actually helping, or making the situation worse?'

Before I could ask what he meant, my tutor had

changed the subject.

The problem is, I've known the man too long. It isn't easy having him 'teach' me anything. And he never lets me slink away without demanding an update on Dad, or making a brief enquiry about me.

At least, it ends up being brief, because it's rare that I have anything I want to share from one week to the next. I'm hardly going to sit at my desk and say I'm not okay because I've got period cramps and the ibuprofen hasn't kicked in yet. That isn't the sort of medically related thing Jordi McAndrew Daley wants to hear.

He'd like a more psychological overview, which I won't give him either. I just tell him things are the same as usual – I wonder if he expects a miracle to have occurred in the seven days since we last spoke – before steering the conversation to his own dad, who was at Edinburgh University with mine around half a century ago, maybe slightly less, until life pulled them in different directions, and then fortuitously threw them back together.

It was how Jordi and I first met. Our fathers re-bonding over their mutual passion for golf and fishing, involving trips to Scotland with their young families in tow, where they could indulge in both pursuits while our mothers kept us entertained. And even though I was closer in age to Jordi's brother Mattheus – Matty, as everyone still calls him – it was the older, quieter Jordi who seemed to tolerate me more.

Their father was in a care home now, the dementia too advanced for his mother to cope with at home. Since Jordi's last relationship ended, I'm not sure he has anyone he can openly talk to about it. Matty might be the more conventionally handsome and polished of the brothers, not that it's relevant, but I've still to find a good use for him. As far as I can tell, his purpose in life seems to be dining out regularly, posting about Michelin Stars or AA Rosettes, and trying to make out he's a foodie influencer. I suspect his lifestyle is still heavily funded by his mum, but it feels inappropriate to ask anyone to confirm that.

I ought to go easier on him, really. London life once had its lures for me, too. And Matty's lived there since he was studying for his degree. Lancaster hasn't been his home in years.

By contrast, Jordi has been emotionally propping up his mum and doing what he can for his dad for ages now. I think that's why his last girlfriend walked out on him, because he couldn't carve out enough time and devotion for her.

I'd never liked her much, from what I saw and heard, but I accepted that he was unhappy when she left and needed time to process it all without me offering my opinion.

With a pointed cough, Polly dragged me out of my introspection, gently easing her phone from my grasp. I'd zoned out and stopped scrolling, she informed me, and she needed to message her mum.

'Oh... Right.' I tried to anchor my thoughts to the present moment. Brooding on the past, however recent, never did much to elevate my spirits. 'I told you, didn't I?' I insisted again, turning my attention back to the newlyweds. 'They're a perfect match. I thought it from the start, when you first mentioned a new man on the scene.'

'You did. I'll give you that.' Polly smiled. 'Nothing to do with the fact the first time I spotted them together he couldn't take his eyes off her. I told you all this and—'

'I'd paired them off long before. You've just got a bad memory. Anyway, it's all documented. I wrote about...' I tailed off.

'Wrote what?'

'Oh, um, my diary. I wrote about it in my diary. So I have proof.'

Her brow wrinkled. 'I know about the diary you've just been asked to do for your writing course, but you never said you kept one before that.'

'Didn't I?' I wafted my hand vaguely. 'Well, it's an

on-off thing. Nothing very interesting, because... well,' I glanced around the large conservatory, 'I don't have much to say.'

I couldn't tell her the truth. I didn't know how she'd take it and I couldn't jeopardise the pattern we'd established, the steady supply of stories.

I knew it was wrong to allude to my issues every time I wanted Polly to stop banging on about something, not that she ever did that much. And it never sat easy with me afterwards. A look of pity, even if it was fleeting and swiftly concealed, was hard to see on anyone's face when it was aimed in my direction.

It wasn't long before Polly regretfully had to go, and I made my way to the kitchen, where I loaded our dirty mugs in the dishwasher, before checking on the casserole I'd prepared earlier. There was enough here to feed Dad and me for a couple of days.

He would come in from golf soon, the leading course in the area bordering our land; what was left of our old country estate, at least. Which was still substantial, by anyone's standards.

As a little girl, I used to walk around the grounds with my grandad, entranced by his stories of Midwynters of days gone by, soaking up the embellishments and dramatic irony.

I don't think we were a bad family, as landowners went. We seemed philanthropic, on the whole, within the limitations of whichever era we found ourselves in.

That isn't saying much, I admit. Years ago, we would have dominated the political and social landscape in the county, and I could have been prouder of that if we'd smashed through the constraints of the day and used our imaginations and integrity to do more.

But excepting the odd scoundrel here and there, we had compassion compared to some of our contemporaries. We could have been tyrannical, never caring about our tenants or employees and using them solely to amass our own fortune or satisfy our debauched needs.

Midwynter Hall, in spite of its grand-sounding name, wasn't as huge as some of those National Trust houses I occasionally got dragged around as a child, only enjoying the experience if my mother let me dress up, so I could pretend to be an actual Lady with a title, rather than a plain, boring Miss.

And I was always relieved my home wasn't a gothic monstrosity, either, though all kudos to those and the chilling tales they might inspire.

There was something whimsical and chateau-esque about the Hall; the way it was all piled on top of it-self rather than taking up a bigger footprint; the garden rambling deliberately, with secret paths and a small maze, stone birdbaths and dainty statues of fairies hidden among the roses and ivy. My ancestors of a couple of centuries ago thankfully hadn't wanted perfectly pruned and manicured grounds.

It was no longer a working estate, though. My great-grandfather had sold off large swathes to a couple of local farmers, and to whoever it was who was responsible for all the greens and fairways and bunkers of the golf course – Dad knew the club's full history, naturally – and Home Farm itself had became independent of the estate just after the last world war.

As an only child, fast approaching my thirties and at this rate destined to remain single, the fate of the Hall once Dad and I were gone was still up in the air.

Distant branches of the family scattered around the UK and further afield, with or without the Midwynter name, would have some claim, and Dad's solicitors were still trying to untangle it all in the increasingly likely event I never produced an heir.

But the upkeep alone to run this place... There wasn't much that was ecological or practical about it. The Hall served little purpose except to look beautiful, even though all anyone could actually see from the road was a distant glimpse of the steeply pitched, lilac-blue roof, with its ornate slopes and angles, over the horse chestnut trees.

Though of course, it was shelter for Dad and me. There were far worse places to be trapped. I wasn't ungrateful. Far from it.

But as Jordi would regularly imply, as he stared out from my laptop screen unsmilingly, why would I strive to fly free, when my cage was so gilded and lovely?

Chapter 2

'You're not hearing what I'm saying. I *wrote* it. I wrote it into existence.' I leaned towards him as if this might help drill it into his skull.

Around a hundred and thirty miles away, in the main living area of an unpretentious but tidy open-plan flat, the elder of the McAndrew Daley brothers blinked back at me, eventually resorting to a surly, 'Huh?'

'I changed their names, in case it ever fell into the wrong hands. But anyone who knows them would instantly see the similarities.'

'Em' – I'd never once heard him call me Emmeline – 'what are you on about?'

He shook his head blankly, and I rolled my eyes Polly-style.

'Polly's friend from Pebblestow, and this friend's boyfriend,' I said. 'Well, husband now. I started writing about their romance as a short story, for the hell of it at first; a writing exercise, nothing more. But as I went ahead and made things up, they started to come true. So I carried on, of course, finishing with a happily ever after at a spring wedding. And – ta-da! – they just got hitched last weekend.'

Jordi kept blinking and shaking his head, without even a 'huh' now.

'You think I've lost the plot, don't you?' I slumped in my desk chair.

'All puns aside, Em, and with the greatest respect—'

'Ha,' I grunted.

'You've lost *something.*'

'So it's just a coincidence that Polly told me things that were happening between them *after* I'd already written it?'

'Unless Polly was stalking this couple, which raises all sorts of privacy issues as well as being downright weird, how could you even know what's true and what's simply supposition on her part?'

'I'm not talking about the tiny intimate details. Only the stuff that's public knowledge – at least within their private circle. Polly's not one of her besties, but they've got closer lately.'

'Whatever you wrote was probably just easy to guess,' Jordi hypothesised.

Did he think I hadn't thrashed this out, night after

night, staring up at the canopy of my bed in wonder and doubt, and whatever else passed through my head when I ought to be in some deep, elusive slumber?

I expected a measure of scepticism from him, though, I shouldn't kid myself otherwise. Considering he was a secondary school teacher by day – or possibly because of that – he was cynical and perpetually tired. Maybe he didn't reveal that side of himself to the students, and stored it all up for the school holidays.

'Have you told Polly about any of this?' he asked.

'Oh, yes. Naturally. And she was all, "Wow, that's so amazing. Can you write a story about *me* now? I really want to find the love of my life in the next year or so, too."'

Jordi regarded me silently again for a long moment, but ended it with his own attempt at an eye roll. Admirably effective, for a grown man. 'You haven't told her.'

'I've known her five minutes compared to how long I've known you. I'm not sure how she'd react.' I couldn't bear the idea of her laughing at me, although she wouldn't do it to my face, and likely not with other people, either, so I'd never know for certain.

'So, you're basing all this on – what?' challenged Jordi. 'One short story? I teach science, remember? I'm not sure I'm the best person to share your fantasies with.' His cheeks acquired a blush, and he cleared his throat. 'Not *those* sort, obviously. I meant—'

'Yes, yes, I know, don't worry. But what I'm getting at is you also teach creative writing, even if it is only in your spare time, and it's always been your true passion. There's no point trying to deny it. Not with me.'

He should have studied English Lit officially, not the STEM route he got funnelled down by his teachers just because he was mindbogglingly intelligent at all that stuff, too.

'I think you're the best person to share this with, Jordi. Your own nerdy passion for literature aside, aren't sciencey folk supposed to imagine "what if?" and then attempt to prove or disprove it?'

There it was. The ruffled brow I was all too familiar with.

'And you know how powerful a force imagination can be,' I added, in a wheedling tone. 'You're always encouraging us to use it more.'

'To write fiction, Em. Which you've already proved you're freakishly good at. Not to get make-believe muddled with fact.'

I felt my nostrils flare. 'If I'm so good at writing already, why am I on this course?'

'You tell me.'

'Because you asked me to join.'

'You didn't have to say yes.'

'You made it very hard to say no,' I simmered.

He massaged his eyes with the pads of his fingers, as if I was exasperating him as much as he was exasperating me. 'I've told you before – only you can answer that question.'

Yeah, yeah, Mr Cryptic. I shifted the subject. 'So, what's the point of this narrative diary exercise you've set us, then? And by the way, you're in it. All our conversations are immortalised, as well as what I truly think of you. So I hope you don't expect me to read it out loud in one of our sessions, or the others might finally twig how well we know each other and accuse you of favouritism. Actually, no. Whatever the opposite of favouritism is, because you're shitty to me compared to everyone else.'

'I'm not shitty with you,' he contested, in a shitty voice. 'What tense are you using, by the way?'

My turn to roll my eyes again. We'd been adults for over a decade now but still had the ability to reduce each other to moody adolescents.

'You know I don't like getting hung up on tenses. I just write what I think sounds best. And I realise this isn't a proper diary, all neatly segmented with dates and whatever.'

'I expect it to read like fiction.'

'So you've told us.'

'But it needs to be truthful. I want you to be honest with yourself.'

'You've said that, too. I hope you want everyone to be honest, not just me. We're all paying the same for your services.'

'Of course.' But his gaze skittered away for a moment.

He was up to something. I knew his 'tells'. Jordi and his woeful poker face. I could typically thrash him at any card game.

'Anyway. Got to go.' He seemed reluctant. 'Early start tomorrow, and I'm knackered.'

'As always.'

'Listen, though… if you want to talk more, I might have some time at the weekend. This conversation doesn't feel over.'

Because it wasn't. I needed him to believe what I was trying to tell him, as bizarre as it sounded.

My voice softened. 'You'll be busy with your parents, won't you?' It was permissible to be mean and snitty with him except when it came to family. And underneath the snittiness on my part and the shittiness on his, there was a genuine friendship that had endured too long to let it fizzle out now.

It felt to me he'd had too many people bale on him, for

a start.

Like his most recent girlfriend. Although admittedly, I'd only had his version of events surrounding their break-up.

But I've always stuck by my conviction that he's a *kind* man at heart; albeit annoying in the concerned big brother role he reserves for me. And if I was in any position to be choosing a mate, kindness would rank highly on my list of must-haves.

Of course, fancying the proverbial (and arguably the literal) pants off someone would be pretty important, too, and I'd never felt that way about either of the McAndrew Daley boys. Maybe because we were too alike on the surface and people we used to meet on those long-ago holidays often mistook us for siblings or cousins.

The Norse-ness of us. Pale yellow hair and skin that wouldn't tolerate the sun with less than factor 30 sunblock. Along with the braces on our teeth back then, and our colourful Boden clothes, there'd been more similarities than differences. Our parents could have been related, too, looking at them; so we must have seemed like one big family.

Jordi was shifting around now, getting ready to end the call. 'I'll ring when I've got a moment, okay?'

He would probably have tons of marking and other

school stuff to wade through. Lesson prep or whatever.

'Fine.' I shrugged. It wasn't as if I had anything more pressing on my hands. Dad would be out on the golf course on Saturday, as usual, if the weather held up. Fitting in another chat wouldn't be a problem for me.

'Bye, Em. Take care.'

I stared at *this meeting has been ended by host* notification, which left me a bit bereft. Another lifeline severed, even if it wasn't forever, but the weeks didn't really go fast enough.

I sniffed, and dabbed at my eyes, although I soon snapped upright. *Enough of this.*

From my vantage point in one of the uppermost rooms of the Hall, I realised night had finally closed in, smothering the countryside in a sumptuous velvet blackness. It was much later than I'd thought.

In contrast to the weeks in between, the creative writing sessions themselves flew by, as did the private conversations afterwards. Today's chat felt unfinished, even though it had gone on longer, and I wasn't the only one who'd sensed that.

Flumping against the stack of pillows in my four-poster a short while later, I accepted I had to collate a larger body of evidence, if I was to have any hope of Jordi believing me.

Chapter 3

·♥·♥·♥·♥·♥·

With a fond smile, I looked across the dining table at my mother, my father passing her the carafe of iced water, while she thanked him in her usual calm and measured way, a gracefulness to her movements I was always endeavouring to emulate.

'Thank you, Henry.'

'My pleasure, Anne.'

My heart pinched, having missed her, even though it had only been a week.

It struck me, studying my parents' interactions as lunch went on, and reminiscing wistfully, that my gift might go back further than I'd realised. Although, for whatever reason, it hadn't actually worked with them.

Perhaps I'd been too young to understand the potential of it back then, which had rendered me powerless to help. Yet even when I was small, I'd sensed something was 'off' about their relationship compared with other couples I must have observed.

It wasn't that they had argued frequently, or neglected each other, or never listened to the other's viewpoint. They'd behaved impeccably in their roles as husband and wife and mum and dad. But there was an element missing I hadn't quite been able to put my finger on, until one holiday with the Daleys, when we'd all been sitting by a crystalline loch as evening set in, enjoying the last flicker of the sun's rays.

Deanna McAndrew, who'd kept her maiden name when she'd married Dean Daley (presumably as they didn't want to be known as Dean and Deanna Daley, but even Jordi hadn't been completely sure) had reached across and squeezed Dean's hand, and he'd laughed and whispered something back, and I'd understood it then for the first time in my life. The Miracle. The Spark. The balance in the equation.

My parents didn't have that. They were friends; they got along; they had a mutual admiration and/or patience for each other's quirks. Their ideas on how to raise me had been evenly matched, united in wanting the best for me and believing they knew precisely how to go about it, which for years had meant the finest education money could buy in our sleepy part of Shropshire.

Luckily, Hartfield School for moneyed young ladies aged four to eighteen, and only about twenty minutes away, had an excellent reputation, so there'd been no need to banish me as a boarder further afield.

On paper, it should have been fine. Except...

They weren't in love.

Maybe once. A love of sorts. Long enough to have settled down, at least. My mother had always seemed at home at Midwynter Hall, but lately I wondered if that was my own blinkered adoration for the house projected on to her. Perhaps she'd *wanted* to feel a deep connection to the place, but couldn't quite manage it, forcing herself to pretend until the day she couldn't fake it any more.

Just after I left school following my A-Levels, my parents had decided to call it a day. Mum had met convivial and successful entrepreneur Randall a couple of years later, at some kind of retreat for divorcees, which had seemed to involve salsa dancing, and they'd announced their plans to marry after only a few months together.

Finally, irrefutably, my mother had fallen head over heels for someone, with every atom of her beautiful being. It was plain when they were together. The ease and comfort in their interactions, the laughter, the passion – *the spark*. And she'd gone to live at Randall's, in his *Grand Designs* style house in the Malvern Hills, all floor-to-ceiling windows and stunning views, and at last looked as if she fitted in somewhere.

Initially, though, when she and Dad had first parted, Mum had moved to the large market town of Bridgely, less than half an hour from Midwynter Hall. While I'd been studying in London, I'd spent some of my holidays with her. But she'd never pressured me to regard her tastefully appointed flat, with its prestigious river view, as a more permanent residence. She knew how much I loved the Hall.

I'd been growing more independent at that stage, though. Flexing my wings. According to my mother, one day I might fly even further away, and never come back except for the occasional holiday.

Mum had painted an exciting and entrancing future for me. This neck of the woods would always be home, she'd promised so thrillingly, over wine on her squidgy sofa or in those little bistros she liked so much, but other homes and an entire lifetime lay ahead.

She'd spread the world at my feet, and I'd listened and nodded eagerly. And when I was out there on my own, I'd gone for it, I honestly had; my main objective seemingly to live up to everything she felt I deserved.

But I'd either tried too hard, or not quite hard enough. I wish I knew.

'How's the writing course going, sweetheart?' Mum broke through my contemplation, reaching across the dining table to pat my hand. 'Is it helping?'

'Mmm.' I resigned myself to being non-committal. 'It gets my derrière on a chair and my fingers on a keyboard. Jordi keeps us busy.'

'That's good. Isn't it?'

'It's better than the alternative.'

'Our Emmeline's doing fine, aren't you, darling?' My father nodded at me, and I felt I had to mirror both the action and the sentiment.

Later that afternoon, while Dad snoozed, Mum took my arm and steered me into the gardens. Although she often visited with Randall, he was away on business now and again; like today.

When he tagged along, my stepfather and my father would fit in nine holes of golf, or sit and talk for ages about putters and birdies and bogeys, with none of the awkwardness people imagined might exist between them.

If Dad had been one for travelling, they might even have arranged a golf trip to Portugal or Spain, and my mother could have stayed with me while they were gone. But Dad hated planes. And trains and automobiles, these days. Though he put up with those if he absolutely had to, which was less and less.

When the weather was dry, Mum liked to spend our mother-daughter time in the fresh air. Sometimes we would garden side by side, tending the roses we both loved, thorns and all. I could remember her working on them when I was little, watching her from my spot on a picnic blanket, the blithest of princesses in my storybook kingdom.

'And how is Jordi holding up?' She guided me along the path towards the compact maze, which I could have mapped out by heart.

Her back was too achy to do any gardening today, and anyway, there wasn't much that needed doing. Between the local firm I employed, and my own less professional efforts, everything was as lush as ever without looking too sculpted.

I'd guessed ages ago that this was one aspect of living at Midwynter Hall that my mother still missed – the freedom to step outside into this splendour whenever she wanted. Randall's garden was small and low maintenance, and although it was all well and good to have an amazing view over an entire valley, when you didn't own all that land and it wasn't your private haven, well then... It could never compete, in my opinion.

'What do you mean?' I said, and stopped walking to let a butterfly flutter past.

'Jordi. Has he adjusted to single life again, or is he still moping? He's always been prone to it.'

'To being single?'

'*Moping.*' Mum shook her head at me. 'But from everything I've heard, I'm not sure he wants to be in a relationship.'

'Of course he does. He wouldn't get into them otherwise. He'd just date casually, like Matty. But it's a while since the last break-up, and on the whole he's fine now. Besides, she'd never officially moved in with him. She kept her own place the entire time.'

'I'm glad he has you – to talk to, I mean – what with everything that's going on with his dad.'

'Well. I don't mind. I'm a captive audience, unless I leave the Zoom meeting; which of course I don't.'

My mother said nothing more on the subject. She'd always had a soft spot for Jordi, like a doting aunt with a favourite nephew. And I knew she talked to Deanna regularly, who she'd once claimed was the sister she never had; but as they'd just come back from some gin-tasting event at a distillery near our holiday lodge, I'd taken that with a pinch of salt. Also, Deanna had a sister already, so couldn't have felt exactly the same.

Anyway, it was easy to buy my mother Christmas and birthday presents. If I wouldn't be seeing her on the actual day, I would just order her favourite botanical gin direct to her door, or a bottle of her signature perfume, which I could smell on her today, in a soothing way. The perfume, not the alcohol. She'd driven here, for a start, in her hybrid coupe, and she was driving back this evening, so hadn't had wine with lunch. I privately suspected that folding herself into that small car didn't do her back any good.

We stopped at the edge of the maze, which buzzed gently with a universe of tiny creatures. An entire wildlife documentary could have been shot in the hedges here, judging by the activity.

As the warmth of the sun lapped over us, I felt sleepy, my limbs heavy. Any welcome punch from the coffee we'd had with dessert had already worn off. But I couldn't let that deter me.

'Mum, do you remember when you first met Randall, and I told you he was perfect for you?'

She looked at me searchingly. 'I remember I was glad – and relieved – when you said you liked him.'

'Yes, but, I *encouraged* you, didn't I? To go for it.'

'You were fine with us dating, as I recall.'

My mother pushed a hand through her short hair, the blonde practically white now, ethereal in the sunshine. She was like some Elven queen in her mossy green dress and matching beads.

'A friend of Randall's,' she went on, 'well, his daughter threw an embarrassing strop recently when he announced he was seeing someone, even though her parents split up years ago. By contrast, you took it all in your stride... my moving out of the Hall, the divorce, my dating again.' Mum hesitated. 'Emmeline, sweetheart, you never made a fuss. You were generous and selfless, and if that's what you want – what you *need* – to hear, and if it helps you in some small way...'

'Mum, it's fine,' I said hastily, aware she felt to blame somehow for my current situation. She always implied it. I assumed it was a maternal thing – the guilt over everything that had gone wrong in my life. But it perturbed me that she felt this way. 'I'm not talking about all that,' I reassured her. 'I meant you and Randall, specifically. I nudged you along in the early days.'

She furrowed her brow. I loved how she could do that and hadn't ever opted for Botox. Her features were so expressive; I never wanted that to change.

'Did you, Emmeline? I never doubted my feelings for him, though.'

'No. No, you didn't. But I'm pretty sure I got you to notice the *strength* of those feelings. And maybe if I hadn't, things might not have progressed as fast as they did, or as smoothly.'

She shrugged. 'Possibly. But I don't see why you're bringing it up now. Today.'

I was trying to establish how my gift might work by gathering more proof. I needed to condense it all into a more rational argument to present to Jordi.

From his point of view (I'd eventually decided to put myself in his shoes) of course it had to sound ridiculous and unbelievable. If I'd weighed it up a bit more before opening my mouth... But I'd felt as if I might burst if I hadn't told anyone what I was thinking, so I'd blurted it all out to him, confident he'd at least listen.

I had no right to be upset by his reaction, though, which had been entirely normal. Jordi didn't have to justify himself to me. It was the other way around. I needed to make the *in*credible, credible.

Should I tell Mum the truth? The words gathered on my tongue. But, no. Not yet. Standing out here in the sunshine, not quite the *cold* light of day but daytime nevertheless, my idea was far more fantastical than when I was hunched over my desk under the ghostly glow of my desk lamp. Darkness was conducive to believing in the obscure and the absurd, whisking you back to those nights when you were a child, reading by torchlight under the covers.

And so, I made some excuse to my mother, hoping it was more plausible than the truth, and we wound our way back to the house, the conversation turning to the minutiae of daily life at the Hall. She might not have been a part of it the way she once was, but she had a vested interest and always would, for as long as Dad or I lived here.

The comfort and familiarity of her perfume lingered when she kissed me goodbye that evening and I wished her a safe journey. I felt her unspoken regret at having to go, knowing I couldn't follow.

'Take care of her, Henry,' she said to my father, with an imploring note.

'I always take care of our Emmeline.' He nodded gallantly. 'And she takes wonderful care of me. Not sure what I'd do without her.'

My mother looked at us both, then up at the backdrop of the Hall, an inscrutable look on her fairy queen face, before she climbed in her little car and drove away.

Chapter 4

·❤·❤·❤·❤·❤·

There was a new gardener among the team. Polly spotted
him first and nudged me to take notice. We were out on
the terrace by the French doors leading to Dad's study,
although not exactly relaxing.

My father, who seemed able to dig out ancient and
obscure paperwork from thin air, like some perverse sor-
ceror, was having one of his regular purges. This mainly involved Polly and me battling with the shredder, a
wicked machine with a will of its own, while Dad dozed
in his favourite armchair by the hearth.

Given half a chance, he would have lit the fire, but it
was a gorgeous day, I contended – our carbon footprint
preying on my mind – and a fire would have roasted him
to a crisp. He'd grumbled at first when I'd thrown open
the French doors, but I'd been adamant. Fresh air never
went amiss at any time of year, even if my father had
to guard against it with antihistamines during hay-fever
season, though somehow the golf club had to exist in

a pollen-free bubble, as he never complained about the perils of being out in the open there.

Sadly, his love of fishing had fallen by the wayside years ago, as had other more minor outdoor pursuits. I would argue with Dad that dust wasn't his friend, either, and a lot of it tended to be found indoors.

Today, he'd stopped quibbling almost instantly, sorted through a stack of unopened mail, then announced he needed a short nap.

Polly and I sat at the wrought iron table outside, with the shredder in the study, near the open door. The best of both worlds. At the sputtering of an engine, my father barely stirred, but Polly jerked her head up to glance across the expanse of lawn. A ride-on mower came into view, and she studied it carefully as it drew closer.

The cottage where she lived with her mum didn't have much of an outside space, so she took a keen interest in the running of the gardens here. She'd helped me deal with enough invoices, and my father and I trusted her implicitly to keep our finances to herself, which perhaps were only as healthy as they were because Dad had scaled back in the years he'd been in charge.

As staff had retired, he hadn't gone out of his way to replace them. Consequently, there were no live-in, full-time employees on the estate these days. One of the last to go had been our housekeeper, not long after I'd moved back – the two things unrelated, as she'd relocated with her fiancé to Eastbourne. Dad, wary of anyone new flitting imperiously around the house, and never caring that he had an image and lifestyle to sustain in the eyes of his cohorts, had wondered if perhaps we could undertake her role between ourselves. Which effectively, I'd come to realise, meant me.

In days gone by, when Home Farm had still belonged to the Midwynters, and they'd had tenants renting cottages on other land we once owned, there'd been need of an estate manager and a small office in one of the outbuildings. But as the remaining acres were mainly for the family's pleasure, and drained the coffers rather than added to them, my parents had dispensed with the estate office soon after they'd got married, and handled any remaining tasks themselves. Living at home again, I'd soon found I was more than capable of assisting my father with those duties, too.

We had an agency who took care of the cleaning, affiliated with a building firm who carried out repairs; while the upkeep of the grounds was contracted to another local company – Leafley's Landscaping & Garden Maintenance – operating as an extension of the largest and most popular garden centre in the area. Leafley's workers were always efficient and professional, and not normally as forward as the young man who jumped off the mower once he'd finished this section of lawn and approached us with a laddish swagger.

A century ago, he might have doffed his cap, but it stayed resolutely on his head as his face relaxed into a grin. His only concession was to nudge back the ear defenders he wore underneath, so he could at least hear us.

He nodded towards the carafe on the table. 'I couldn't have some water?' he asked, with none of the deference he might have shown in another era, which of course I'd never lived through except when I got totally swept up in my favourite episodes of *Downton Abbey*.

I often imagined myself as a blonde version of Lady Mary, complete with the severe 1920s bob that my dad's barber, one of the few people who ever came regularly to the Hall, had been coerced to tidy up after I'd hacked at my own hair in a fit of despair. He'd maintained it ever since, realising he could confide in me about his other clients, and I would listen and sympathise and never spread a word of gossip.

Anyway, this young man in his green Leafley's polo shirt with matching cap, had already caught Polly's attention before he'd even leapt off the mower. He was new, and much younger and less weather-beaten than the others.

I frowned, even as Polly grabbed the spare glass we'd brought out for Dad and set about pouring.

'I forgot to bring a bottle,' he said, after downing it. 'Sorry.'

'More?' asked Polly, her hand still poised on the carafe.

'Thanks, this is great. It hit the spot. Sorry for disturbing you.' He didn't look apologetic. That lopsided grin was annoying. And he wasn't budging. Just standing there, blinking amazingly long lashes at Polly.

'I'm Zac.'

'But no Efron,' I muttered under my breath.

'Polly,' said Polly. 'Hi, Zac.'

It was no surprise to see him zoning in on her. With her flawless rosy cheeks and flicky ombre hair, in combination with her warm demeanour, she instantly put me in the shade. Not that I couldn't turn it on when I wanted. I'd secured my fair share of attention once, when I'd been in the mood to be flattered.

It wasn't anything as crass as vanity that had me bristling with irritation, but the simple fact my friend could do so much better than this boy with the cheeky chappie air and dangerous, crooked smile who obviously thought too much of himself and probably wouldn't think enough about her. Not in the way she deserved, at least.'

She needed to stop her own lash-fluttering pronto, or she'd be in trouble. The air positively crackled with sexual chemistry, which I could just about recall from some distant liaisons of my own that had never quite fulfilled their initial promise.

I scowled as they both hungrily swiped right in their heads. From what Polly had told me about her love life, she was an expert at making the wrong choices at the worst times with the most feckless of men. She got swayed too easily, she'd confided. And I could see her melting before my eyes right now, and not because the sun was high in the sky, or the fact that there was no soft, cooling breeze ruffling the air (which actually made sorting through papers much easier, as they weren't trying to take off from the table every few seconds).

'Right. Well.' I poked my chin in the air, Lady Mary style. 'The rest of your team are probably looking for you, Zac. From what I know of Bob Leafley, he doesn't like slackers.'

The tanned face with the few well-placed freckles turned towards me in obvious amusement. 'No... No, you're right. Bob prides himself on professionalism at all times.'

'If you get thirsty again,' piped up Polly, 'you know

where to come.'

There were probably a dozen innuendoes there, and she was practically drooling as Zac pulled out a Leafley's business card from the pocket of his tight, stone-washed jeans.

'And if you ever need my services...' He grabbed a pen from the table and scribbled what I assumed was his phone number on the back, before passing the card to Polly.

If he even hinted about being an expert at trimming bushes, I would vomit. But thankfully, he just broadened his smile, which was devastating enough. Poor Polly. She had no chance. Not unless I intervened.

As soon as he was out of sight, I turned to my friend, who had the card clutched to her shapely chest. That was as far as Zac would get, I decided. This had to be nipped in the bud before she made another decision she'd regret. I owed her too much.

'You're not really going to call him, are you?' I demanded.

Polly's gaze skittered away and wouldn't lock with mine, much like Jordi's the other night. Jordi. Hmm. A shame he lived a distance away and had so much on his plate. He would make a reliable and more intellectually stimulating boyfriend than anyone Polly was likely to meet around here. It wasn't the first time the notion had flitted through my head. Although, he couldn't seem to hold on to women, so maybe there was a dealbreaker I wasn't aware of, lurking behind that Thor-like exterior.

'Why not?' Polly asked, her brow puckering slightly. 'Anyway, I'll probably just text – to start with.'

I'd never likened Jordi to a Hemsworth in my own mind, but Polly had mentioned it once, when she first saw a photo of him. It was a bit disconcerting that I could see what she meant now, whereas I hadn't at the time. I suppose it was comparing him to this Zac guy, who wasn't my type at all. But then, neither was Jordi. Although I wouldn't kick a Hemsworth out of my bed if I ever found one under the duvet.

I frowned.

All by the by. I was losing focus.

'He was cute,' she was rambling on, 'and I'm not after anything serious at the moment, anyway.'

She'd made that claim before, but I wasn't convinced. People typically said it when things weren't going well and they wanted to save face.

My father coughed and stirred, and I pushed back my chair. 'I'd better get him a *clean* glass.' I trusted my tone of voice to make it clear to Polly I wasn't pleased with her. 'He could do with a drink himself, and I only brought out three glasses.'

She didn't look as abashed as I'd have liked. Her gaze had wandered back across the emerald lawn, probably hoping for another glimpse of the brazen Zac.

My granny on my father's side would have called him a fly in the ointment.

For my friend's sake and her long-term happiness, he was definitely something that needed squishing.

Chapter 5

❦ · ❦ · ❦ · ❦ · ❦

'...So, you see, I *do* have some freaky ability to dictate the course of a love affair.' I smiled smugly into my phone, having FaceTimed Jordi on the off-chance he was free.

He'd texted a vague excuse for not calling last weekend, and I'd made a stellar effort not to pry. He'd been caught up with 'family stuff', and if he didn't want to talk about it that was fine; I was well aware how difficult it was for him. I had plenty of my own 'stuff' to discuss, which I'd been doing for the last five minutes.

'What more evidence do you need?' I ended on a challenging note and waited for his reaction, suppressing a rebellious voice in my head demanding to know why he couldn't have called me another time – it needn't have been restricted to the weekend – and why I'd had to take matters into my own hands.

As I suspected, he wasn't up to anything exciting. A waste of a breathtaking evening, because the view of the setting sun in Lancashire from his window seemed as glorious as the Shropshire one was from mine. But instead of savouring the outdoors, we were both at our desks.

He rubbed his brow, under his tousled mop of hair, his expression shielded. 'You're not going to let this rest, are you?'

I didn't see why I should when it was as plain as day there was some truth in what I was trying to tell him.

'Em,' he said, and I wondered why the shortening of my name always sounded different when he said it; why it made me sit up and take notice, even those times when I didn't want to. 'Do you really believe, just because you also wrote a story about some woman who works in the toyshop in Pebblestow,' Jordi said slowly, haltingly, 'and some bloke she's been seeing, the fact she's just moved in with him is indisputable proof it was all your idea?'

'Well, it's the second couple in Pebblestow I've helped.'

'You say "helped", others might say "interfered".'

I bridled at this. 'That's a very unhelpful response. It's just... the things I write about... they tend to come true. At least when it comes to romance involving real-life people, because I wrote about world peace once, and *pfft*, you know how that's going. It was speculative, before you ask – the world peace story.' I flapped my hand dismissively. 'Not worth showing you. Besides, I don't think it's just when I *write* romances, either. I helped orchestrate Mum and Randall getting together.'

'Encouraging your mum to get serious with a bloke she already liked is hardly some ground-breaking magical ability. Marrying him was just one of several outcomes.'

'I wouldn't say it was the likeliest one, though. A lot of people don't want to rush from a divorce into another marriage. She was worried, and I had to persuade her *not* to be. In so many ways she was happier than I'd ever seen her.'

'When you were a kid, Em, didn't you want your parents to be... closer than they were? I know they didn't argue, but... something wasn't right.'

'I – I suppose so.' I shifted in my chair.

'So then,' he said, more gently, 'why didn't that come true?'

It wasn't a pleasant thing to admit, the fact my mother hadn't been as content as she could have been while married to my father. But I truly believed neither of them were to blame for the lack of compatibility. It was just one of those things. A gradual shift, like the continents drifting apart. But perhaps they never noticed how irreversible it was until it was too late; and maybe, if I'd known back then that I could directly influence the course of their relationship, I could have done more.

Was this knowledge, this possibility, the driving force

behind my mission to do things better now? To make the most of my 'gift'?

I didn't think it was solely about wishing for something to come true. There had to be more to it. My parents might not have been a good match in the first place, only they hadn't seen it; or the fact they'd rushed into it meant they'd fooled themselves that they knew what they were doing. Mum was so different when she was around Randall, she practically sparkled. Had she merely *settled* for my father, unconvinced there was someone more suitable out there?

I wondered all of this out loud, almost as if Jordi wasn't listening and watching. He was so quiet, he might as well not have been there, except that it was somehow simpler to talk aloud and speculate, knowing I wasn't on my own.

When I was small, I'd had a teddy called Roly, excellent for comforting snuggles – until I'd lost him in a park and been inconsolable for weeks. It had been easier to confide in my cuddly bear than when I was without him, internalising everything as I got older and unable to voice my distress.

Minus the snuggling, it was odd that Jordi might be the equivalent of my furry confidant these days. Speaking of which...

'Are you growing a beard on purpose?' I interrupted

my flow to peer harder at my phone screen. 'There's a lot more fuzz on your face than usual.'

'What? Oh.' He rubbed a hand along his jaw. 'I don't know.'

Come to think of it, the man actually looked scruffy. Not that Jordi was one for excessive primping and preening; he'd always been low maintenance compared to his brother. But at the very minimum he kept his hair trim, his stubble under control, and his clothes ironed. Today he looked like he might have skipped a trip or two to the barber's, and resorted to raiding the laundry bin for something to wear.

'What's wrong?'

He narrowed his eyes. 'What do you mean?'

'I'm nattering on and on here, when there's clearly something up with you.'

'Nothing's wrong, Em.' His tone softened. 'I appreciate your concern, but you don't have to worry.'

'You're not still pining, are you?'

A weird catch in his voice now. Maybe he *was* upset about that. 'Pining?'

'For her. Rosemarie.' I knew full well it was Rosamunde. 'You were too good for her.'

There, I'd said it. At last.

His expression flattened. 'How would you know?'

I shrugged, not so confident in my next statement, as I ignored his question and continued: 'Also, I don't think you were as invested as you think you were.'

'Shit, Em. You have no idea how invested I am. *Was*,' he added quickly, which didn't escape me.

The great lump still had feelings for her. Poor eejit, as my granny on Mum's side would have said. To be so hung up on someone so apathetic to his plight. There had to be more I could do.

'I wish you lived nearer, Jordi.'

His gaze flicked back up to mine. 'You do?'

'Then I could be an actual physical shoulder to cry on, rather than a virtual one. Mum said she thought you were prone to moping, but she meant it in a nice way. She frets a lot over people she cares about.'

'That's a fairly human instinct. But how is moping ever nice?' he countered.

'The moping itself isn't. It was the sentiment behind what she said. Anyway, there's someone here I think might be perfect for you; it's just a shame—'

'Don't.' He put out a hand. 'Don't write me into any of your stories, not even experimentally. I don't need you to manufacture a happy ending for me.'

'No, but, listen. You know Polly—'

'No, I don't,' he said sharply. 'I don't know her. I know

of her, and that's as far as it needs to go. And I appreciate she's been a really good friend to you the last couple of years, but don't suddenly start getting any hare-brained notion that she's the perfect woman for me or something.'

'She might be a whole lot better than the ones you pick for yourself.'

'Yeah, well,' he shifted in his chair, 'you might be right there.'

I reeled slightly. It was a big deal whenever he admitted I was right about anything, especially when he put it as plainly as that. Muttering, 'Oh,' I scuttled on, making a promise I probably had no intention of keeping because, like my mother, I had his best interests at heart, too. 'Anyway, I won't write about you, except for this diary thing. I'll let you wallow in your own misery for now. I think Mum's right – you do enjoy moping.'

'Maybe. But we've all got our faults. Even you, Em.'

'My father doesn't think so!'

The man on my phone screen didn't bother to laugh; not even a tiny chuckle. And when I yawned out of nowhere, he immediately followed suit.

'Seems as if I need an early night,' I said. 'Get some rest yourself, Jordi. You look like you need it, too.'

But after we'd said our goodbyes, I didn't follow my own advice. An idea whirling, I turned to my laptop, lifting the brushed-metal pink lid with a new reverence for its power – and mine.

Determinedly, and with an eager (and selfless) heart, I opened a fresh Word doc.

Chapter 6

Raindrops dribbled down the leaded pane. Such a stark contrast to the last few days of unremitting sunshine, which had coordinated so well with my more positive outlook. Where was the sunshine and my sunny mood now?

Holed up inside, curled up like the cat I never had (blame my father's fears and allergies) on the window-seat in my bedroom, I traced the drops on the glass with the tip of my finger. My spirits were damp and dreary, but in a restless sort of way, like butterflies in my stomach navigating a dense fog.

I was probably just missing Polly, and more detached from reality than I could comfortably cope with.

Whenever she came to visit, she typically cycled over, or her mum dropped her off. On the odd occasion, when we'd had a girls' night, she'd stayed in one of the guest rooms. Polly didn't have her own car and didn't partic- ularly enjoy driving, anyway. At least she'd learned and passed her test. I'd always put it off. Too stressed and busy with my A-levels at first, and then in London I hadn't felt the need when I had buses, the Tube, or black cabs at my disposal.

I'd said to Polly not to bother coming today because of the weather. She'd ended up getting an extra shift at the café in Pebblestow, where she'd worked all the time I'd known her. A lot more use to her than visiting me. Her bank balance never saw any benefit when she simply came over in her capacity as a friend. Much better this way.

A notebook lay open on my lap and my pen was chewed at one end. An awful habit I'd never grown out of. Poor pens and poor teeth. But the page in front of me was still blank.

Why was freewriting like this so hard?! The way Jordi encouraged us to do it, ideas were supposed to flow from our subconscious and all we had to do was capture them, however nonsensical they seemed in the moment, picking out the ones that made sense later. But nothing was flowing, unless you counted the rain. Did rain flow, or did it strictly only fall? My pen tapped against my mouth, and I tried hard not to open my lips. The pen had a life of its own, though, and sneaked through.

Striving to clear my mind, it only felt fuller, drifting back to a couple of evenings ago when my fingers had barely paused as they'd flown across the keyboard, the beginning of a new story taking shape. Jordi had asked me not to, but I couldn't help myself. Why shouldn't I do something nice for him? If he was as sceptical as he made out, he wouldn't expect it to come true, so what did it matter? I wouldn't tell him, though. If it worked, he'd find out soon enough.

My breath hitched a little. It was ambitious in scope compared to anything I'd attempted before. Or it seemed that way. I knew better now how much weight and potential my words carried – was that why it felt different?

I'd had to stop, however, and admit I was tired; plus the story needed breathing space. It was just a beginning.

It had to come true.

But, oh – if it did!

And I'd realised as I lay in bed that night, I couldn't rush it. With each choice I made, there were too many paths shooting away from it. I had to be sure I was picking the right one. Not too much detail, either; just enough so that the story and the propelling forces made sense. The motivations had to ring true. It wouldn't do to be too random.

But anyway, the notebook. I turned my attention to the empty page again. Jordi encouraged his students to distance themselves from technology whenever they could, and get back to basics. Just a writer and their pen. Nothing fancier. It was supposed to unblock us somehow; tap into something primal – the same creative impulse which once produced cave drawings, perhaps – but I often struggled to make it work the way he intended.

Perhaps I wasn't great at honesty. How did you freewrite about 'the truth in your heart', anyway? This latest task was ridiculous. I frowned at the notebook. My heart had to be as full as the next person's, but I didn't know how to transfer it to the blank page. Where did you even start with something so immense? The heart was a bottomless abyss full of fears and regrets and...

Could I get away with that? Write what I thought a heart *ought* to contain? And if so, I'd started off pretty bleakly.

> *Jordi, this is pants. You suck. I hate you.*
> *Help me though.*
> *Arghhhhhhhhh.*
> *I'm being extreme, I know. But what's the point of this?!!!!*

My pen scribbled away. At least I was writing something, even if it was veering off topic. For half a minute, I was in the moment, writing what I was feeling. So that was truthful in a way... wasn't it? Bordering on the negative, admittedly. And I was thinking too hard again. This exercise was about *doing*. Getting words on paper and analysing them later.

I threw down my pen in frustration. *Stop this, Em.*

All I was achieving was trashing Jordi, and it could turn into a major rant if I let it get out of hand.

I needed a distraction.

Resorting to my phone, I went to the class WhatsApp group.

> Does anyone have a clue what 'the truth in your heart' is supposed to mean? And how does it relate to the diary assignment?

I was being obtuse on purpose. A risk worth taking for any crumb of helpful advice.

As I anticipated, responses came fairly quickly. There were a handful of fellow course-mates who seemed to live for the 'thrill' of our meetings and assignments and the online chatter in between. Which wasn't a put-down. My life these days was hardly any buzzier.

> He just wants to make sure we're mining

> as deep as possible, Em. Our deepest
> selves need to shine through. Plunge
> into your very core. We mustn't try to
> hide, even from our darkest, wildest de-
> sires. After all, this is just for us. No one
> else will read it. Now's not the time to
> be shy!! Let it all out.

My eyebrows shot up, though none of that was out of character for Nancy-Jane. I was convinced she had designs to write erotica.

Hetty was next. Older than the rest of us, and her mother's long-term carer. I pitied her, in spite of despising pity when it was aimed at me. With a sigh, I skim-read her contribution. As always, Hetty was gushing with her praise and language.

> Jordi would never dream of setting an
> assignment if it didn't add value to this
> course. He's too conscientious for that,
> and too intelligent and nice to mock us.
> I kept a diary when I was a girl, and it
> taught me a lot about myself, and when
> I read it back now I always think good-
> ness what did I know? I had my head in

the clouds. I thought my life would turn out quite differently, but things happen for a reason, Mum always says, and fate has a way of changing your dreams into something else. But I never complain. Because I wouldn't be here now, would I? Learning with all you marvellous people, though some of us surely can't have anything much left to learn. In spite of all your questions, Emmeline, I'm certain you're secretly asking for our benefit, not your own. I can't believe otherwise, my lovely. Really, you're already a star...

I stopped reading, unable to deal with Hetty's fangirling when it got out of hand.

After another heavy sigh, though, I braced myself and scrolled to the next response.

Not sure about this diary business myself, TBH. I'm paying to learn about structure and technique and all that other stuff. If I wanted therapy I'd pay for it. If no one's reading it except us, how can we be critiqued? How can we f-ing learn??

Hello, Frankie. Bloody well say it like it is, mate.

I concurred with him to a degree, though. What was the use of writing for ourselves, without any constructive criticism? We didn't have to pay anyone if we wanted to do that. No direct debits or PayPal.

> All writing is practice. Have you ever kept a diary before?

That was Cole. Good old Cole. Always in search of harmony.

> No I haven't. But my point is: I didn't need to pay someone to tell me to write one. If I'd wanted to do it I'd have done it ages ago. For FREE.

Frankie plainly didn't feel he was getting his money's worth.

My brow stiffened into a frown. Should I warn Jordi? It felt like snitching. This group had been set up for the students. Most of them seemed to really like Jordi. Frankie was an outlier. A very attractive outlier. But I didn't want to concede he had a point simply because his cheekbones had something of a vampire about them and his dark eyes seemed to burn into my hazel ones every time he stared out from my laptop. He always made me tingle inside, even though he was looking at everyone and not just me. Was everyone else tingling, too?

I didn't have to wait long for Cole to respond again.

> Writing can be superficial or deep or somewhere in between. Jordi just wants us to go deep for this one. To understand what that really feels like. And the person we ought to know most is ourselves. We need to tap into that every time we write a lead character, because maybe we can't make them human or relatable enough if we don't put something of our own humanity into them.

Cole sounded as if he were trying to talk Frankie down from some ledge. But suddenly I wondered if Frankie was just scared of writing what was in his heart, and using all this bluster as an excuse.

If I was reading him correctly, he was an angry young man, still railing at the condition that had shrunk his life to his apartment, however stylish and modern and functional it looked on our screens. Too fatigued and in pain to venture very far physically, and often mentally and emotionally, beyond his front door. Society didn't always seem to want him there, anyway.

He'd probably had a string of girlfriends once. Now he had a succession of paid carers. And his aunt, too, who owned the flat. I could sense his beholden-ness made him even more frustrated. He seemed stuck at that *why me?* stage.

What if we were all stuck? Or some of us, at least? But could you ever move past it completely, or was it always too easy to slip back into despondency? Was Jordi trying to help us find the messiest and most muddled bits of ourselves, and lock them down on paper? Ultimately, to improve our writing. Flesh out the new protagonists and antagonists we hoped to create one day. Make them less like cardboard cut-outs and more morally grey, more realistic.

He'd never said why he'd given us this assignment. Jordi seldom explained the reason behind his tasks. He just set them and let us unravel it for ourselves.

If I'd worked out the overarching point of this one correctly – and it had taken me long enough – then I hadn't done what he wanted. Not really. I'd gone about it in a cursory way, documenting my existence without giving it proper context. I knew *how* things had gone wrong for me, but I'd never properly faced up to *why*. I'd never felt ready.

Was Jordi trying to test if I was strong enough now? If we were all strong enough?

I appreciated he was approaching the course differently with me than with the others. He'd more or less said so privately at the start. The rest were newbies; or at least, lacked my experience in the industry. Whereas I'd had my chance; my debut; my grand entrance. And I couldn't help thinking the others felt more entitled to their turn in the spotlight.

I could almost feel them patting me on the head in a condescending fashion, aside from Hetty, who in spite of her faults seemed genuinely kind. *Step aside, Emma de Wynter* (my old pen-name), *and let us have a go, hun. We deserve it more than you. We won't waste our chance.*

And however amiable they were with me on Zoom or in the WhatsApp group, however much Jordi tried to reassure me, or however much I tried to reassure myself – I still felt like I shouldn't be there, struggling to rekindle something I'd allowed to die out.

The Passion. The Spark.

Because I'd never been 'in love' – except with my

writing, my craft. Boys and men had always paled by comparison. But somewhere along the way I'd fallen *out* of it and tumbled headlong into something else entirely. Writing had been so much a part of my identity that when I forgot who I was, I forgot how to write. And so I'd run back to the only spot on earth where I'd ever felt truly safe and wanted.

The house that had inspired my stories in the first place.

Chapter 7

Once upon a time, I was a respected author in a commercial sense – living the dream desired by so many novelists, and wannabe novelists, all around the globe, longing to see their work on the most coveted bestseller lists.

It hadn't happened solely by chance; I'd worked hard for it while also studying for my master's. But the rarest of good fortune had been involved, I couldn't deny that. Others with more talent had floundered purely because luck wasn't on their side. For me, though, everything had fallen serendipitously into place, and throughout my early twenties I'd led a glittering, seemingly charmed life.

I wouldn't say I'd taken success for granted, but maybe I hadn't prized it as much as I should have or respected it enough to remain vigilant at all times. Failed to fully understand the pressure involved to stay on the giant hamster wheel until I'd flown right off and landed on my backside in a shocked, tangled heap.

Long before that, though, since as far back as I could remember – when there'd been no downside to my dreams – I'd been entranced by the combination of stories and magic. My favourite books, still among my favourites now, had had elements of other worlds beyond ours woven through them, and small lives caught up in epic adventures. Alice and her Wonderland. Dorothy and Oz. Lucy Pevensie and Narnia.

As a child, I was convinced there had to be a portal to a secret faerie realm right here at Midwynter Hall. It was the sort of house some authors I admired liked to write about. For a start there were tales carved in pictures in the oak panelling of the great hall and gallery. Possibly local legends that could never be translated because there was no one left who remembered them. Or, more likely, a story made up by some ancestor with the same storytelling gift as me. Desperate to make sense of the images, I came up with my own tales, like a graphic novel. Copying the pictures and weaving my own narrative underneath.

If I'd had siblings, I might not have had to fall back on my imagination to keep me occupied. But the closest I ever got to that were the holidays with Jordi and Matty, and I used to moan ironically that having a needy little sister trailing after me all the time would have been preferable to occasional forced proximity with gangly boys, whose feet reeked of cheese no matter how many cans of

Lynx they got through, leaving me coughing and choking in their wake.

Named after Dutch great-grandfathers on their mother's side, I had to admit they'd seemed exotic at first, partly for being males. Educationally, in some ways, I'd been deprived. Hartfield School wasn't co-ed, so I'd mainly only mixed with girls up till then. The fascination wasn't mutual, however. The McAndrew Daley brothers socialised with plenty of (popular) girls at their own school, and according to Matty I was boring and nerdy by comparison.

Jordi had learned to put up with me. He would never have called me vapid, because I frustrated him too much and kept him on his toes, but that was better than being overlooked, and he seemed to understand that. A different character altogether to his brother and into reading, too, with a sense of humour that conveniently complemented mine, eventually we were sharing books and Matty was calling us both nerds, although I couldn't shrug it off as easily as Jordi seemed to.

The brothers had still regularly gone off to enjoy testosterone fuelled pursuits, however, like white water rafting, which probably helped repair their bonds when they were stretched thin by constant fraternal squabbles. My mother, far more intrepid than me, would tag along too, slotting right in with the adrenaline junkie crowd.

Jordi and Matty's mum had been content to stay back at the lodge. We'd often gone for long walks, following bubbling, frothing brooks and laughing over funny shapes in clouds, and I'd thought she was lovely and she'd said it was nice to have a girl around for company. She'd taught me to bake and sew, which were hobbies my own mum, who preferred the outdoors, had never shown much interest in.

When I thought of Deanna McAndrew now, I felt overwhelming sadness, picturing her with the man she loved so fiercely, no longer recognising who she was sometimes and lashing out over it. And I would wonder, on his side, where love went when you couldn't remember who you'd ever felt it for, and how tragic and perpetually heartbreaking it was to go through that every day, for both of them. The isolation. The waiting, knowing it was only going to get worse.

And I couldn't stop thinking how awful it was for Jordi. My heart seemed to ache hardest for him. Probably as he shared snatches of it with me, letting down his guard at times, before he hurriedly jammed the mask on again, claiming he didn't want to burden me because I had enough going on in my own head. My imagination had to fill in the rest, and I wished I could do more for all of them.

But I was stuck. Figuratively. Literally.

Because the thing is, when I'd flown off the hamster wheel, Dad had insisted I move back in with him so he could take care of me. And I hadn't hesitated giving up my rented studio flat and my London 'friends', who had stopped calling me as much, or at all, anyway.

I'd fled to Shropshire, publicly announcing it was for my father's sake but knowing it was more for mine. He had recently stepped back from his consultancy work, whatever that had encompassed, something to do with wealth management, and was clearly bored and lost – in truth, he was only lonely when he wasn't at the golf club – wilting away on his own in that too-large ancestral home, which I could now admit I'd missed like a child missing a beloved parent.

I knew the Hall loved me back. It had welcomed my return as only a cherished home could. Houses have that ability. Nothing can convince me they don't absorb some of our DNA over time, perhaps from the dust we help create. Maybe the shedding of dead skin isn't such a disgusting notion and there's more to it than just biology. Of course, not so good if you have allergies.

But that's not the point. I'm not sure what point I'm trying to make. I know how lucky and blessed I am to have grown up here. Whether all that cosseting led to some of my issues, I don't know. I won't let anyone pick at my brain long enough or hard enough to make sense of the chaos.

Not even dear Polly.

Now how did *that* come about – a friendship so strong and sincere, when I haven't left the estate in so long? This might be part of the 'diary' I could let Jordi read one day, because he doesn't seem to want to understand how much Polly's company has meant to me, claiming it's one more reason for me not to want to get better. In his opinion, she's made things too easy for me. But he doesn't get it.

When my friend leaves, when she goes back to that life she paints so vividly for my benefit – the job at the café; the nights out in Bridgely, even the ones that end badly; the cottage where she lives with her mother; the village where old-fashioned community spirit (unashamedly strong) neutralises the gossip (rife, and not always accurate)... whenever she goes back to that world... I can't follow.

I can't be a part of any of it, regardless of whether I want it or not.

So if I had a choice, as Jordi seems to think, why would I bring that on myself?

Anyway. I was in danger of digressing. Again. I'd decided to focus on friendship as a starting point for all the 'truth in my heart' business. And perhaps it would make me more grateful, on the whole, to remind myself how an angel like Polly had found her way to Midwynter Hall in the first place – just when I'd needed her most.

It had all begun around two years ago.

My father had claimed he needed to get someone in to assist him with his infernal paperwork. The mystery of how one man can generate so much of it, especially in this digital age, remains unsolved. I'd been dealing with the household side, while he dealt with the rest, refusing to bother me with any of it until he brought out the shredder, convinced I derived satisfaction from feeding that temperamental machine.

So, even though he'd officially retired, he still had investments and other small concerns, and had asked his accountant to recommend someone who could come in for a few hours a week to help him keep on top of it. Someone trustworthy and discreet, who wouldn't mind helping with other 'little' jobs around the house outside the remit of our regular cleaning firm, such as helping me sort through the attic rooms.

It was a task I'd decided to undertake out of boredom, which had soon turned to curiosity as I'd picked out gems from among the junk, dispatching antiques to a local auction house and interesting bric-a-brac to various charity shops in Bridgely, and sadly consigning things to the tip if they were beyond repair. Or – my favourite – finding a spot for something exquisite and intriguing within Midwynter Hall itself. Giving it a new lease of life. A renewed purpose.

When Polly Evans had turned up – Dad's accountant lived in Pebblestow and knew Polly's mother – she'd taken me by surprise. I'd been expecting some retiree like Dad, with time on their hands, and a need to occupy their mind rather than being motivated by money.

Instead, at the front door, fifteen minutes late, I'd found a young woman around my age or a bit younger, in skinny jeans and a tie-dyed hoody, rosy-cheeked in a healthy way, unlike me with my too-flushed blotchy face – and desperate for the extra cash. Although she worked in a local café, the owner hadn't been able to increase her hours back then.

'No disrespect to Sallie or the café,' Polly had confided, over a pot of strong tea she'd insisted on making, though my father had slipped away with his mug to his study, 'but I don't want to be a server for the rest of my life.

And Sallie owns the business, while I'm just an employee. I appreciate that it's stressful, but I'd like my own business one day, too. If I can figure out what I want to do exactly.' And she'd sighed dramatically and frowned out of the window, cupping her hands around her mug.

'Did you say servant or server?' I'd wondered if my ears might need syringing, like Dad's a few months earlier, but then I put her words into context. 'You meant server, didn't you?'

'It's more neutral and inclusive than waitress.'

'I suppose. Though, debatably, I think anything with "serve" in it comes by some route or other from the Latin for slave.'

'Really?' She'd blinked. 'Unfortunate.'

'A lot of language is probably unfortunate if you go back far enough. Anyway,' I'd rattled on, 'with servant, you can add subcategories, like maid, or footman, or valet. Sometimes there's a need for specificity.'

'You've been watching too much *Downton.*'

'*Downton Abbey*?' I'd shrugged. 'Goes without saying, doesn't it?'

So that was it. We'd bonded over Yorkshire Tea – the only sort my dad liked – and our adoration of an iconic TV programme. I'm not sure we were the target demographic, but that hadn't stopped us devouring every episode.

Polly had gazed around the Hall's large kitchen. 'This place is beautiful,' she'd said with genuine admiration. 'Nothing like the kitchen in *Downton*, though.'

'It would have been, once. Nowadays, it's a lot glossier than I would have personally chosen.' I'd explained how my recent ancestors' tastes didn't quite match my own, but that over time, I'd been putting my own stamp on things.

'I can't imagine calling a place this size home.' (Still spoken with an air of wonder.)

'I can't imagine *not* calling it home,' I'd said fervently.

She'd studied me over her mug, then, and I'd squirmed under her scrutiny. 'No disrespect, but you're not what I'd imagined.'

I could have said the same about her, but I'd been too caught up in what she meant.

My hair had been long back then, probably scraped back in a pony-tail, and if I remembered correctly, I'd been in stained leggings and an old denim shirt. Having abandoned the department store make-up and the chic wardrobe when I'd fled London, I hadn't yet started to devote time and effort into my appearance again.

'I'm seldom what anyone expects.' I'd shrugged.

'You're posh on the inside.' Polly hadn't said it in a

nasty way. Even at that early stage, I'd sensed there wasn't a mean bone in her body, or in any cell, come to that.

'I'm the product of an expensive education and a pampered childhood.' She might as well have the blunt truth. No reason to delay it. 'There's not much else to me really. I'll admit I'm not as posh as some people I've met. But I'm probably what certain sections of society mean by the term "snowflake", in its more modern sense.'

There'd been a long pause, and then Polly spoke again.

'You're agoraphobic.' Again, there was no harshness to this. She'd only said it matter-of-factly. 'That doesn't make you a snowflake. And I never get that analogy, anyway. Snowflakes are amazing. If you zoom in on one, it's sparkling with magic. And when you have enough of them, they transform the world outside your window.'

'They cause a lot of disruption, too,' I'd pointed out; my throat tightening with emotion, because Polly must have read my last novel. She'd more or less bounced one of my own character's words back at me. Not that other people hadn't ever said the same, in slightly different ways, but we didn't have to make a big deal of that. Maybe she was a fan of Emma de Wynter's *Hate Me Love Me* series, or maybe she'd just done her research.

'Like that's a bad thing sometimes?' Polly had argued. 'Because the world's so great as it is?' She'd pushed back her chair and set about clearing the table. 'Be a snowflake as much as you like, presh, as my mum would say. I'm not being paid to judge anyone.'

And she'd gone off to find my father, to see what her employment entailed, while I'd sat with my thoughts and realised she wasn't really here for him.

She was here for me.

Chapter 8

·❤·❤·❤·❤·❤·

There's a lot more folklore than you might think surrounding tea. You could get snarled up in it for hours. But one of the more positive notions is how sharing a strong brew can denote the start of a new close friendship.

This didn't come into my head, sitting across the table from Polly that first day. I was only reminded of it recently, stumbling across an Instagram post with a quaint stock photo of a teapot and dainty china cup. I couldn't have predicted how important her visits would become. I'd been stung by so-called besties ghosting me when my life had unravelled. I wasn't about to throw myself at Polly, begging her to be my friend.

But friendship had bloomed, and with a pang of foreboding, as the recent confetti blossoms blew away and the days grew warmer, I worried our sisterhood was about to be tested.

Her life – and mine, unsurprisingly – had been mostly stagnant since we'd met. Polly still wasn't sure what she wanted to do as a long-term career. And I was still flitting around the Hall; although nowadays, for all intents and purposes, the semblance of a contented chatelaine.

Much had changed when it came to how I present-ed myself, though. It was one thing to dress in sloppy clothes on purpose, another just to let things slide be-cause you couldn't be bothered. Gone were the stained out-of-shape leggings and shirts, along with the straggly tangle of straw-like split-ends.

Polly and I now shared skincare and make-up tips, and even though I never went anywhere, or received a multitude of visitors, I was nearly always neatly dressed, flowy in summer and woollier in winter, with a touch of colour-correcting primer, lip-gloss and mascara and the sense that if I took some pride in myself, if I invested in *me* physically, the rest might fall into place.

Eventually.

Eating nutritiously was a given, because I cooked for Dad and myself, and made sure we had a healthy vari-ety, along with more traditional English comfort food; the sort Dad remembered fondly from school dinners, involving stodgy suet and sticky jam.

Dad stated he couldn't survive on the Mediterranean Diet alone, like Mum claimed to when she wasn't tucking into our roasts, and as his regular rounds of golf provided him with exercise, I let him off.

When it came to supplies, I tried to source as much as I could from local businesses, so long as they were happy to deliver; particularly the nearest farm shop. Polly often brought treats from the café, too. Cookies and cupcakes, and the most incredible mince pies in the lead-up to Christmas.

We lived well, but not extravagantly. I made use of everything, at times more inventively than others. Keeping the Hall at its best was an accomplishment, though I'd closed off rooms we never used; cleaning and heating them was too wasteful.

Maintaining what was left of the estate, only the gardens now and some parkland, also fell willingly on me these days. Dad had no interest in green things unless there was a hole with a flag sticking out of it.

It was therefore my fault we'd hired Leafley's Landscaping and Garden Maintenance, back when our old gardener retired and his nephews, who used to help him, moved away. So, it followed that it was also my fault that Zac Not-Efron had come into our lives, soon to become a blot on the horizon that only threatened to get bigger.

Polly turned up one day looking flushed in an emotional capacity, rather than just those rosy accents in her cheeks, and as soon as we were alone in the conservatory, out of earshot of my Dad, she blurted out the reason.

She'd been texting with Zac. It didn't matter who'd started it, she said dismissively. But I reminded her he'd given her his number, not the other way round.

'Yeah. Okay.' Polly pulled a face. 'But he's really cute, Em.'

'You've used that argument before.'

'I'm not after anything serious.'

'You've used that one, too.'

'But it's true!' she protested. 'I don't want to get involved with anyone. I don't need a boyfriend. They might hold me back, or tell me things are fine as they are; or want to get serious and have kids instantly or something. Some men do, you know. Until they don't.' I knew she was referring to her errant father.

I softened. 'But you don't hate your life…?'

'Hate's a strong word. And, no. I don't. I have a lovely mum, who never mithers me. Two decent bosses, and yes, of course I mean your dad as well as Sallie. I live in a cottage to die for, even if it is tiny and Mum has a *lot* of stuff, so there's not much room for mine. But that's all right. It stops me hoarding crap, too. And I have some great friends.'

'You're including me?'

'Of course!'

'Okay,' I sniffed. 'But I think you're trying to side-track me.'

'I didn't *have* to tell you that I'm going out with Zac on Saturday night.'

'You hadn't told me that. You just said you were tex-ting.'

'Yes, well. We arranged to go for a drink in Bridgely. Nowhere fancy, just that small bar I know.'

I sighed and shook my head. 'Poll, you've been here before; blindsided by some guy with an above-averagely pretty face.'

'Zac's different.'

'Besides the fact he works for Leafley's, what do you know about him? What's he told you?'

'So far? Not much, other than his full name's Zachary Martin, but—'

'You've been messaging. He must have said something more. How do you know he's not married, or he hasn't got a serious girlfriend?'

Her eyebrows swooped into a frown. 'Is that your first thought? Are you really that paranoid?'

'No. Well, a bit. But it's happened to you before. You told me yourself; it's not as if I heard it on the rumour mill.'

'I *am* your rumour mill,' Polly reminded me. 'So what

are you saying? That I'm only capable of attracting cheats or weirdoes?'

I put out a hand, urging her to calm down. 'I'm only going by what you've told me. I've never seen any of these men for myself – have I? Maybe if I had, I could have warned you off.' I paused for dramatic purposes. 'But I have met Zac.'

She groaned, and I sensed her wavering. 'He's different... I think.'

'Listen.' I rubbed my hands across my knees, innocently averting my gaze. 'At the end of the day, this is your decision. If you really believe he's not going to mess you around, or that you're going to be able to keep your emotions out of it, then go have a laugh; whatever that involves. If no one else thinks it's a bad idea, then I'm probably paranoid, like you say. It's not as if I've dated in ages, is it? So what do I know?'

'You're not a novice. You dated back in London.'

'I suppose,' I sighed.

'And you said some of them were turds.'

'Affluent rather than effluent, though. Jordi would point out one's an adjective and the other's a noun, but you get my point.'

'Maybe that's colouring your opinion?'

'It might be; to a degree.' I frowned again. This wasn't

going quite the way I'd wanted, but I couldn't seem to stop making things worse. 'They can't all be as bad as each other, can they? Or is it just men of a certain age? Or just men? In general?'

'I'm not holding my breath I'll have better luck than my mum. Right now, though, I don't need to find anyone special, even if he exists. I've got too much I need to figure out on my own. But, you know, I wouldn't mind a bit of fun, especially if it's with someone I really fancy...'

'Like Zac?' I gritted my teeth.

'I'll be careful. I mean, I'm not silly. I know how to take care of myself.'

I frowned through the window into the sun-drenched garden. 'He's infuriating, but Jordi's not a turd. I wish you could meet him. I think you'd get on.'

'You're biased. You don't actually know what he'd be like as a boyfriend.'

'I know what he's like in other ways. I think that counts. He'd really like you. *And* he's available. You ought to be his type whether he knows it or not. You're a lot better than the sort he usually falls for.'

'Thanks.'

'That was a compliment.'

'I know what you're doing, Em. But Mr Amazing-ish isn't here. Zac *is*. And I promise not to make a numpty of myself.'

It wouldn't matter what I said; she was too determined. I had to give in, or risk it leading to a row the likes of which we hadn't had before. It didn't sit well with me but I had no choice. If I bided my time, it might come to nothing, anyway. Maybe he'd stand her up, or coolly call it off at the last minute without explanation.

Not that I would wish that on anyone, and especially not Polly. She'd had enough to deal with. What with that guy, Trev or Trey, I couldn't recall, who'd been sleeping with two other people behind her back. Or the one who'd seemed really nice, Elton Something-or-other (but not John), who kept inviting himself over for tea at her place, when all along he had a thing for older women and it was her mum he'd actually fancied.

I'd heard it all from her own lips. And if it had happened during the time I'd known her, I'd provided the proverbial shoulder to cry on.

'Fine.' I flicked imaginary specks from the strap of my dress. 'Go have your "fun", then.'

Polly regarded me with a bemused expression. 'What are you doing?'

'Just dusting off my shoulder,' I said primly.

'Why—' She stopped and frowned. 'Oh.'

'Oh,' I echoed, and went off to make tea, ensuring I

didn't brew it too weak, because according to folklore, that meant you'd *fall out* with a friend.

Chapter 9

He still looked rumpled and unshaven, the shadows around his features worryingly pronounced. As I stared at the screen, hand resting on my chin, I picked up a curious tension between him and Frankie and remembered I hadn't warned Jordi about the mini WhatsApp rant. Then again, I would have felt guilty staring into Frankie's hypnotic vampire eyes if I'd dobbed him in.

I was the *Twilight* generation, and clearly hadn't matured.

The lesson tonight was entertaining, though a tad embarrassing, with Frankie being all sweet and attentive to me, praising my work more than ever, and our hairy tutor growing ever more sullen.

But I ended up feeling bad when it was over, faced with Jordi on his own. I hoped the sullenness wouldn't be redirected at full force in my direction and he might at least try to shake it off. I wanted to get to the bottom of his dishevelment without excessive grumpiness on his part.

I was worried his dad had declined even more, but Jordi assured me there was no change and that his mum was okay, too, thanks for asking. He somehow made it sound as if I *hadn't* asked. Hmm.

I found it hard to imagine he was *still* missing Rosamunde. She'd exited his life a couple of months ago, maybe longer, and he'd seemed to be over it. Or had that just been wishful thinking on my part? Did some people relapse the lonelier they got? Was that it? Had she really left such a massive hole in his life?

To divert him, and dispel the tense and uncommon silence that set in between us, I told him about Polly's impending date with Zac.

I'm not sure what I was hoping for. Jordi was hardly going to get jealous; he hadn't met her in person or ever communicated with her. I couldn't expect him to react the way I would have liked, all bothered and blustery. And he didn't. Instead, he turned it around on me with no effort whatsoever.

'You're not happy about it, because you're worried what might happen if Polly gets serious with a bloke.'

My turn to go, 'Huh?'

'You'd probably see less of her. Polly's other friends seem fine with her visiting the Hall regularly—'

'She works for my dad,' I interjected. 'And what's it got to do with anyone else, anyway?'

I was aware Polly kept her other friendships separate from our own, and I didn't question it. I preferred it that way and chose not to probe deeper. She might be trying to protect me somehow, but I didn't want to risk having that confirmed.

'More often than not, she's there just to see you,' said Jordi. 'From the sound of it.'

'You're talking out of your backside. Anyway, she's dated now and again since I've known her, and I didn't react like this then.'

He shrugged. 'I wouldn't know. You and I weren't in contact as much. Not like now, at any rate. I mean, we used to talk, but...'

'Happier times,' I quipped, before it struck me that Jordi had been busy back then with Rosamunde, and I might have inadvertently reminded him of that.

On a few occasions, when he'd been beta testing his online course at a seriously reduced rate, agonising that he didn't have the credentials to teach creative English at that level, his then girlfriend had 'accidentally' popped up in the background, instantly looking apologetic, laughing in her tinkling fashion and saying his flat was too small to fit in so many people.

The joke had soon got tired, and I'd wondered why she didn't just spend those evenings at her own place.

'Hiya, everyone!' She would waggle her fingers at the screen. 'Hiya, Emmeline, how's things? Jordi's so happy you agreed to take part in this beta thing. I can't tell you how glad I am you haven't given up on it yet. He's not so bad a teacher, is he?'

And I'd smile at her tensely and think:

a) *this is really unprofessional. Poor Jordi.*

And b) *I have never actually met you in the flesh, person-who-needs-to-learn-how-to-use-bronzer-properly, please stop acting as if we're family.*

I hadn't seen it lasting between them, there was something so inauthentic about her, and my hackles had risen for Jordi's sake.

I could only pretend to be sad that she'd broken up with him.

'I'm not the possessive type,' I said now, folding my arms.

'I wouldn't know.' Jordi folded his arms, too.

'I mean with friends, as well as men. Or even with men who are friends. Everyone's entitled to go out with whoever they like. It's just, I have a very good sense of who's right for someone and who isn't. So I simply feel it would be in Polly's best interests for me to intervene. I'm not doing it out of jealousy.'

'Right,' he grunted. 'So come on, then. Rosamunde and me – did you always think we were doomed?'

My eyes widened. I hadn't been expecting this. Swivelling on my pink velvet office chair, I focused on my pinboard, smothered in random motivational quotes that seemed more meaningless every time I looked at them.

How to respond diplomatically?

'I was never *entirely* sure that you gelled,' I said slowly. 'She was all right, in her own way. But I'm not sure she was a good match for you. Which is why I think Polly—'

'Bloody hell, Em.' He unfolded his arms and pushed away from his desk. 'It's not going to happen, okay? For a start, I'm here and you're there. Both of you, I mean. So you can't set us up. I don't want an online or long-distance relationship right now. Especially if I've never actually met the woman. And I wouldn't want to drag anyone into my life, anyway, just to inflict my crap on them.'

'What crap? Jordi, is there more you're not telling me? I'm happy to be dragged into it, because I'm already part-way there. If you offload on me, you don't have to bother anyone else. You can date for pleasure and let me take care of the rest.'

He frowned for a long moment, shaking his head.

'That's really immature, if altruistic. But it doesn't work that way.' The arms were folded again. 'Everything's fine, Em. It's just school stuff.'

'Nothing about you is screaming *fine* to me. And there isn't anything immature about wanting people to be happy.'

'No.' He blew out air through gritted teeth. 'But it's the way you go about it...'

'Unconventionally?' I wasn't going to bring up magic again, though. My current story had stalled. Nothing was happening the way I'd written it. Doubts were more than just creeping in. And he was right. He had a life, and it wasn't exactly around the corner. Aside from his time studying in Cardiff, and then in the US for a year, he'd always lived in Lancashire. His roots had to go deep there, even if his present flat was only rented.

'Misguidedly,' he said, by way of correction.

'Well,' I fished about for something to say, to perk him up while taking the heat off me, 'it'll be the holidays before you know it. You can rest and recharge. A change of perspective can help.'

He didn't respond.

Ominous.

'Do you have plans?' I probed, trying to sound nonchalant. 'Obviously I've booked myself into Chez Midwynter. Third year in a row. There's a sunlounger out there with my towel on it already.'

Not even a small laugh. Instead there was a definite grimness about him as he muttered, 'I was meant to be going to Sardinia with Rosamunde. I booked it as a surprise for her, for Christmas. Before Dad got worse.'

Damn. I'd walked right into that one, on more than one level.

'It's okay,' he went on darkly, 'don't panic. She's still going – with her new bloke. She paid extra to amend the ticket.'

'Phew.' I pretended to wipe my brow. 'You had me worried! Please don't scare me like that again.'

He snorted. 'She had the decency to check with me first.'

'I hope she had the decency to pay you back for the holiday, too.'

'Well,' he hesitated, 'she covered his share, but she said hers was my gift to her. Which it was. I didn't know what else I could do. A bit late now, anyway. I just want to forget about it.'

'Sorry for bringing it up,' I said, sufficiently sheepish. 'You're too much of a gentleman, Jordi. I'm no lady, though. If I'd known about it, there's plenty I would have said to her.' I felt dutybound to get us off the subject.

'Expecting to see Matty at some point?'

Now Jordi looked even more dour, if that were possible. 'He'll probably come to stay with Mum for a few days, and visit Dad for a couple of hours. That'll be it. To be honest, I would have felt guilty going off to Sardinia and leaving Mum on her own. I can't rely on Matt to step up.'

So it was 'Matt' now, was it? The old childhood nickname relegated to our golden past. Well, I wouldn't be able to relinquish it so easily.

How did we get like this?

The thought came to me suddenly, bringing a lump to my throat. Me, agoraphobic and trapped. Jordi, jaded and stuck in his own rut. We'd never imagined this for ourselves, those long days spent dangling our feet over the jetty by the holiday lodge. When he wasn't being a pain, he'd seemed so funny and wise. A rock-like presence, keen to do so much good in the world.

Looking back, I'd felt totally safe with him, and I couldn't say that about many men I'd met since. I'd even trusted him enough to send him excerpts of my writing while he'd been off at uni, aware he might mock me for five minutes before hopefully offering reassurance and his own brand of refreshing honesty.

I'd kept his encouraging replies in a special folder in Gmail, and still read them now and again, in a wistful way, reminiscing about the girl I used to be. It was torture, to be honest, even though I told myself I needed to face up to how I'd felt once, how chock-full of promise. Perhaps, if I could recapture that feeling, that enthusiasm after acing my GCSEs and launching myself into Sixth Form...

'Have you had it out with Matty?' I steered myself back into the conversation. 'It sounds like you're just letting him get away with it.'

'He's too flaky. Mum doesn't need that.'

I thought back again. There'd been a time when Matty and I had run into each other a fair bit when I was in London. We'd both studied there and stayed on afterwards. He'd fallen in with an even more pretentious crowd than mine, but they'd curiously overlapped at parties. It was easily done, I remembered: falling in with people in a superficial sense. Matty had always sought glory in some form or other. But, like me, he was nearing thirty now, too. Had anyone actually tested how responsible he might be, given the chance?

I didn't want to press Jordi on it. Not today. Family could be a tough subject at the best of times. Easier to move on.

That probably meant drawing the call to a close, though. Our conversation felt strained, and my eyes were growing bleary. I blinked to clear them. 'Right. Well. I'd better let you get off, then, seeing as it's a school night.'

'Hmm.' He flipped his gaze away.

'Just ring if you ever want to chat, you know. Or message me. You don't have to save it all up for these sessions. It's not as if I'm out and about living the high life. I'm pretty much always available. *You're* the busy one. You git,' I added, in the hope it might raise a smile.

But to my mounting consternation, he couldn't even manage a wry one.

Chapter 10

· ♥ · ♥ · ♥ · ♥ · ♥ ·

The sun was struggling to break through a swathe of dense pewter. Thanks to a brisk northerly breeze, there was an unseasonable nip in the air, too. Though saying that, it was hard to know what was considered seasonable any more.

Mum and Randall had both made it over today, and my mother and I had shooed the men off to the driving range while we cleared up after the Sunday roast. But my mind wasn't on the task; or on my mother, chattering away.

Despite my urgent messages to Polly, demanding she spill the tea about her date the night before – 'tea' used here in an idiomatic sense; I'm not still banging on about folklore – the only response I'd received from her, so far, had been to say that she was fine, not to worry, and she'd talk to me later.

I'd asked for proof of life because, for all I knew, Zac could have got hold of her phone and managed to hack into it somehow, and was now in the process of reassuring all her important contacts that Polly was safe and well.

She'd sent me a shaky video back, but it was definitely her, sans make-up or filters, not that she needed any, drinking from a giant reusable Starbucks cup.

With just a blank cream wall behind her, I wasn't sure where she was. Not her cottage. There were no blank walls there, as testified by the pictures I'd seen, her mum having an uncanny knack of filling any vacant spots with colourful artwork she'd managed to pick up at craft fairs or markets.

'You're distracted, sweetheart,' observed my own mother, loading the dishwasher. 'Is something wrong?'

'More than usual, you mean?' Terser than I'd meant to be, I apologised before filling her in on the latest. 'So you see,' I concluded, 'this Zac guy is bad news. And I feel... helpless, I suppose.'

'Don't you think you might be going overboard?' Mum spoke slowly, carefully. 'Polly's your age, isn't she?'

'Nineteen months younger, actually.'

'Right. Still very much an adult, though.'

'Yes. But when did that ever stop anyone from messing up?'

'True,' said Mum. 'I just meant, you can't take responsibility the way you might with a child.'

'It was Polly herself who told me her judgement's

flawed when it comes to men.'

Mum rubbed my arm. 'Are you jealous, Emmeline?'

'In what way? Because Jordi accused me of that, too.'

'Did he?' Her hand dropped back to her side. 'And did he explain what he meant?'

'He thinks I'll feel left out if Polly starts spending more of her spare time with a new boyfriend.'

'I see. Well, that wasn't quite what I was trying to say.' She hesitated. 'Sweetheart... do you have feelings for Polly? Is it okay to ask? I don't want to be accused of prying.'

'You think I'm jealous because I'm in love with her?' This wasn't illogical, but I shook my head. 'It's not like that.'

'For your sake, I'm glad. Unrequited love... it's never easy.' She stared off pensively for a moment. 'So, your only concern is Polly might end up getting hurt herself?'

'Y-es...' I began tentatively. 'Okay, *no*,' I conceded, with a sigh. 'Jordi wasn't entirely wrong. I am a bit apprehensive about the impact it might have on things. But honestly, Mum, if I thought for one second Zac was right for her, I'd be cheering her on. And I know she'd still make time to come here because the right guy would never stop her. He'd be sympathetic and understanding and—'

'Are you sure this noble, selfless man isn't just a myth? You sound hard to please.'

'Well...' I might as well say it, 'Jordi would be a good match. In fact, I've told them what I think. But they won't listen.'

Mum's brow lifted. 'Jordi? And... *Polly*?'

'I know, I know. He's not exactly local. But stranger things have happened. I think if they could meet – in person first – they'd really hit it off. And then,' I shrugged, 'well, they could make it work long-distance, to start with.'

Mum pulled out a chair, her expression thoughtful again as she sank into it. 'You don't think it's risky – for you?'

'In what way?' I pulled out a chair myself.

'They wouldn't want to be apart like that forever, would they? At some point, one of them would have to think about relocating.'

'Polly would never leave her mum. They've lived in Pebblestow for years.'

My mother frowned across the table. 'So, what then? Can you see Jordi living around here?'

'I – I hadn't thought that far ahead. I just had them going out, and all the excitement that goes with the long-distance thing. Meeting half-way for mini breaks.

Late night video calls. Thoughtful little gifts arriving out of the blue...' I sighed in a dreamy fashion. Living vicariously wasn't so bad when you had some control over it. 'The romance of it all, you know?'

'But if they're so well matched, they'd want more than that. The novelty of trekking back and forth wears off.'

Why was Mum splitting hairs so much? Overthinking this?

'Eventually,' I sniffed. 'There'd be no rush. Polly's still got a lot she needs to figure out when it comes to life goals. As for Jordi... once his dad's gone...'

Maybe Deanna would want a fresh start herself, somewhere new. But I didn't want to share my musings. Some of them were too sad.

Plus it made me oddly self-conscious to admit I wouldn't mind Jordi living closer to Midwynter Hall; to have him here on tap.

He could make Polly happy, and vice versa. I was categorically convinced by now that they could be great together. Even if no one else seemed to see it.

And teachers – well, they could work anywhere, couldn't they? There were schools within easy commuting distance. Jordi probably wouldn't have much trouble finding a new job in the area.

I didn't divulge the rest of my ideas to my mother,

though. They sounded logical in my head, but I dreaded how silly they might seem out in the open. Because all my problems typically arose when I attempted to explain myself to others. What had once seemed obvious to me would suddenly have me questioning myself, and doubting, and hiding away where it wouldn't matter.

So, if I didn't have to function in a hostile environment, if I could live a perfectly good life without criticism – or worse, without anyone really knowing the real me, because I put on such a great show I even fooled myself...

I reined myself in. It wasn't the right time to delve too deeply and indulge in any of that 'truth in my heart' business. But it was hard not to. Which was infuriating, as I didn't have my notebook, and my mum was watching my every move in that sly way that means she cares unconditionally.

Parents – the good ones – view us differently from everyone else. That's just the way. They want everyone to view us like that too, to see what they see, but at the end of the day they can't protect us from *everything*, not the way instinct compels them to.

Was that the hardest part of being a mother or father?

It was likely I'd never know; not first-hand.

But I did know that every moment, in countless ways, humans put themselves in the way of approval or disapproval; love or hate; good and evil.

From that first day at school, to our last day in the skin we call home – we're being judged. I don't mean by some omniscient being or anything along those lines; not in this instance. Just that, regardless of the fact we all live in glass houses, we're still throwing stones left, right, and centre. We can't seem to help ourselves.

It's back to DNA all over again, I suppose. There's no getting away from it. We're ridiculous creatures.

'You know what I always say.' My mother picked up the thread of our conversation after a telling silence. 'Many a time, life gives us what we need, not what we want.'

And I was back in the room again, blinking at her across the table, wondering what I needed or wanted, and what this had to do with Jordi exactly. He seemed wedged in my thoughts more often, and I hated seeing him so miserable and pathetic and unkempt. That wasn't him. He'd never been that person. He deserved a Polly in his life. Pollys were rays of sunshine in a gloomy world. Jordi needed someone like that, regardless of what he'd told himself.

Perhaps I ought to double down on my efforts. The story I'd started writing about them had stalled, but it was up to me to make it viable again. For their sake, I had to have faith. I had to channel the confidence and purpose and brilliance of Emma de Wynter, wherever she'd gone. Because, for a time, that woman had been fearless and fierce.

And she'd never taken no, or even maybe, for an answer.

Before Mum and Randall left that day, my mother asked to speak to my father privately. They disappeared into his study for a full half-hour, while my gregarious stepdad tried to keep me entertained with stories of his travels and the hedonism of his youth, in the hope it might provide inspiration for a book one day. Randall was always regaling me with anecdotes and wild yarns, and possibly a few of them were true.

While I was often amused, today I found it hard to keep up with him or stay focused. My mind kept drifting to the study.

Were my parents talking about me?

But why now? Today? Nothing much had changed. I was still where I'd been a week ago. A month ago. Even a year or more ago.

There was no pressing reason to discuss me behind closed doors. My mother phoned my father often enough for updates if she had to miss one of her weekend visits. Dad was never discreet when he took those calls; he let it be known that I was safe here, and cherished, and he was keeping an excellent eye on me. I don't know what my mother expected him to say.

When at last they came out, Dad was nodding pensively, and Mum looked as if something had lifted, which made me uneasy, as I hadn't noticed she'd been quite that burdened before.

In a cloud of perfume and hugs, my Elven-queen mother was whisked away by Randall, and the rest of my Sunday played out as it often did, with Dad challenging me to a game or two of cards, before he dozed in his favourite chair and I took myself off upstairs to slump at my desk and scowl at my laptop.

Today, I didn't slump or scowl, but allowed my fingers to fly across the keys.

In a place like Midwynter Hall, magic could never be far away. The child in me had always known that. And what if I had absorbed some? A tiny portion, as reward for my devotion? What if *this* was the root of my 'gift'?

I couldn't squander it, could I? So, I wrote without holding back.

Without doubts or despondency.

I wrote as if my life depended on it.

Chapter 11

· ❤ · ❤ · ❤ · ❤ · ❤ ·

It was Monday when Polly finally got back to me properly, though her tone was neither abashed nor apologetic.

But everything was fine, I reassured myself. I had this in hand. However fabulous it all seemed now, the scales would soon fall from her eyes and she would be right where I'd positioned her in my story.

Ripe for being rescued.

—Before you get all judgey (you do, so don't deny it) YES I did stay over at his place, but NO we didn't do anything. We were just having a really good evening. He lives in Bridgely. It was easier to go back to his than asking my mum to pick me up. And obviously cheaper than getting a taxi on my own. I'd missed the last bus. Zac lives with his mum and sisters before you ask Xx

—So you had the spare room?

I was sceptical, but kept my fingers tightly crossed.

—Not everyone has a spare room, Em!! But we didn't rip each other's clothes off either. And he went out the next day before I woke up and bought me the best latte ever from Starbucks. Seriously I think it's from a secret menu only Zac knows about. We ended up spending the day together before he drove me home. It was late and Mum wouldn't stop talking and asking me stuff, by the time I went to bed I just crashed. I meant to message you back. Sorry Xxx

He sounded too good to be true. Or maybe it was more a case of Zachary Martin having honed his act and knowing how to lull his prey into a false sense of security.

Admittedly, it seemed he'd already got her where a lot of men ultimately aimed to get a woman, and he'd managed to resist the urge to pounce. That didn't necessarily mean he was one of the good ones. Zac *might* have tried his luck but stopped when Polly didn't consent. He didn't need to be applauded for basic decency. Also, he lived with his mum and his sisters. Hardly a love den, then.

Still. Had Polly been naive? I didn't know these days. I felt detached from the whole singles scene, and not just by circumstance.

—Are you seeing him again?

I braced myself. But she didn't answer immediately, so I got on with pottering around the kitchen, neatening things up and putting bits and bobs back in cupboards. Polly might have jumped in the shower, or she might be busy getting ready for a shift at the café, or simply living her life in some other way that didn't involve justifying herself to a meddlesome friend.

I frowned out of the kitchen window into a day that felt as surly as me, leaden and unwelcoming, devoid of all the joys of spring.

When my phone pinged, I fumbled to scoop it up.

—I had a good time and I want to see him again. But I told him I don't like pressure. I just want to keep things low-key. And where he's at right now, he

feels the same. Might go for a walk or
have brunch somewhere next weekend.
Anyway I'll be seeing you before. Talk
then. Got to run, need to be at Sallie's
by 10. Xx

Wondering whether this merited a reply, I looked up
as my dad wandered in, phone pressed to his ear and a
mug in his hand. He spotted me, did an about-turn, and
walked out again.

My frown deepened. 'Do you want another coffee or
tea?' I called after him. 'I can make it...?'

He didn't answer, though he'd probably heard me.
Unlike him to act like this. He wasn't keen on phones, for
a start, and avoided talking into them unless he had to,
although he'd mastered texting. Compounded with the
private conversation with my mum yesterday...

Anxiety prickled all around me, like a shield designed to
keep me safe but mis-programmed at some point in my
life to turn inwards and attack me instead. I couldn't let
it get out of hand.

Not dissimilar to negotiating with a hostile force, I had
to be one step ahead. Cleverer. Armed and ready if things
went wrong.

Prepping myself, in raincoat and boots, I stepped into

the courtyard. Hard cobbles underfoot, yet every bump felt grounding and solid. I was so bound up in the love-liness and expanse of this place, it was instantly soothing.

My world felt huge. And compared to so many other worlds, it was.

I couldn't deny my privilege.

This was my sky, however grey and rain-filled it looked today; my gardens, my trees, my terraces. Beyond the gates, at the end of the long drive out of view of the house, there was a different sky belonging to everyone else. I'd been there. Lived beneath it. Felt it pressing down on me, suffocating and immense and cold. The entire weight of a terrifying, terrible world. And I hadn't been able to shrug it off.

Even when I reminded myself others felt it, too, and many of them were okay-ish, they coped – they didn't end up locked away like some princess in a tower, though mine was a self-imposed isolation – even when I told myself all that, it never helped.

It made no difference what I said, or what anyone else was quick to say. I might be confined by my own mind here – but at least it was home. It was *safe*. And therein lay the first stumbling block, according to Jordi.

I was apparently too swaddled in a utopia of my own making. Expending so much effort shaping it to look just the way I wanted, I didn't have any energy left for my writing, or for fixing everything that had gone wrong. In his opinion, 'avoidance' was an easy strategy to employ, because I'd created the best spot on earth for myself, to do all my avoiding in.

Would it have been different, if I hadn't had Midwynter Hall?

Of course. But what that might have looked like...

Well, that was anyone's guess. Even Mr Know-It-All didn't have the answer to that one.

It had all started with a simple panic attack. Probably nothing simple about it, if I'd ever given a psychologist the chance to analyse it, but too late now. Standing in the beauty hall of a Bond Street department store after lunch with my editor and agent. I'd had two glasses of wine, and was feeling mildly giddy and happy, I think. Surely I was happy.

We'd been celebrating the fact I'd signed a new book deal. All hush-hush for a while still. But it was a big one. Of course. *Naturellement.* I was a rising star. An ingenue. Already shimmering brighter than I felt my output deserved, but there it was, it had happened. I wasn't going to let anyone down, least of all myself. Everyone was already bursting with pride at my achievements. They'd told me so, repeatedly.

Being Emma de Wynter was a big deal. She had an air of quirky glamour about her, even when she was lounging around her bijou flat, surrounded by fairy lights and little fake cactuses and Frida Kahlo prints. Her hair was pale gold and tumbled, Rupunzel-like, in soft waves down her back. She never ventured outside without make-up, but she'd perfected it to look as if she wasn't wearing much at all, hiding those stress-induced rosacea flare-ups.

So there she was that day, wafting like an exquisite perfume herself, sniffing swanky scents with her up-and-coming agent Isabella, who'd taken her under her wing when she'd signed her and become like a big sister really, being only a few years older – when suddenly Isabella had vanished (not literally; just around a corner) and Emma de Wynter had found herself alone. And in those few seconds, stretched out into forever, her heart had hammered and her throat had constricted and her head had spun, and she'd almost keeled over from the tightness in her chest, and the fact her vision had blurred to a mere dot in front of her.

With minimal fuss, though, Isabella had reappeared and got her home. They'd shrugged it all off as overwork;

Emma de Wynter's last deadline had been gruelling. And then Isabella had dashed off for her first date with the suave American lawyer Emma had nudged her towards when they'd been out one night. The suave American lawyer Isabella had subsequently married and settled with in Los Angeles, having given up literary agenting in exchange for selling ridiculously expensive Californian real estate, popping out a perfect set of twins, and taking pictures of her labradoodle – or something oodle – for the dog's very own Instagram account.

But that alarming episode in the beauty hall hadn't been an isolated incident for Emma de Wynter. She'd soon found it harder and harder to go out on her own, and had endeavoured to always have someone on hand to accompany her. But the embarrassment on her part, and the excuses on theirs, had become too much for her.

It had been easier, she'd decided after being let down for the fourth or fifth time, not to venture out at all. Practically everything she needed could be delivered to her door. Much wiser if she just got on with writing her next book. Socialising was for other, less industrious people. She didn't depend on it the way they did.

Except, the next book hadn't happened, either.

Day after day of staring at a blank screen had likely triggered the first panic attack at home. Or it might have been the lack of sleep. Or all the caffeine she'd seemed to consume. Or the fact that her publicist kept nagging her about not returning her calls. Or that the divorcee with the greasy comb-over, from the flat below, had always been lurking in the shared hallway when she'd come downstairs to collect a delivery, making the sort of comments that led her to wonder if she'd need a restraining order one day. Or just that she missed Midwynter Hall, and hadn't stopped missing it all the time she'd been in London. Or – worst of all – that Jordi hadn't been in touch in ages, not even to remind her that her ego didn't need pandering to, while attaching a silly selfie as he pointed to her last book still charting high in his local Tesco.

Too much. Too soon.

That was what people had said. She couldn't remember who, exactly. It was just bandied about; overheard as if through a fog. Success had cost her dearly. Demanded more than she could pay. The price had been too high. Blah, blah. Whatever cliché was in vogue that day.

There probably wasn't much sympathy from certain quarters. Emma de Wynter had shut down all her social media accounts, preferring the trolls that lived under bridges and tormented random goats, or the haters that just hated cauliflower, or cheese, or just cauliflower cheese, rather than the ones who hated people (specifically people who weren't men) and made their feelings as public as the socials allowed.

Emma de Wynter had shed her skin and left it behind in that flat with the Frida Kahlo prints, and the fairy lights strung above her desk, and the mini cactuses on the windowsill. But the problem with shedding your skin was finding you didn't know who, or what, you were left with.

The whole point of coming home to Midwynter Hall, at least after the first phase of humiliation and misery, had been to find out.

Emma de Wynter's bank account was still topped up with royalties from her earlier contracts – the publishers having recovered the partial advance for the books that never materialised – though she rejected any calls from her editor, and her email responses were polite yet firm.

The final deal had been torn up; or whatever the terminology was, as she hadn't physically ripped any papers. It might have been cathartic if she had. No, she wasn't ready to write more of the same. Too bad if her novels were being talked about with increasing frequency again. Emma de Wynter wasn't on the socials. She wasn't on anything. Well, except for those antidepressants for a while, to keep her mum happy.

Emmeline Midwynter, on the other hand, had a new Instagram account – albeit incognito – but that was mainly to follow Polly, always delightful and gossipy in her sweet way, and Isabella's dog (@poochy_tales_from_lalaland_xx).

Aside from that, her account was private. There were kittens in her feed, and sometimes otters. And ads for make-up and cosmetics.

If her reclusiveness only added to Emma de Wynter's celebrity, the person she was now wouldn't know, and pretended not to care. And it was rare for anyone in her small circle to ever dare mention it.

Chapter 12

Frowning, I came to a surprised halt in front of a small white van, 'Spick Span & Sparkling' emblazoned in a swirly font down the side.

It wasn't so much that it was an unfamiliar sight on the estate, merely that it was parked in front of the modest limestone lodge at the end of the drive, instead of up at the house.

Also, it wasn't our cleaners' usual day.

I'd taken to going on long walks the last couple of afternoons, varying the route each time. This was the first occasion in a while that I'd followed the winding drive all the way to the main entrance.

Donwell Cottage – once the Gatehouse, before it was renamed in honour of a long-serving and much loved groundskeeper, long before I was born – had been empty for ages; since our last groundskeeper had left. It stood, as its former name implied, close to the iron gates with their fancy scrollwork that gave on to a leafy country lane.

A magnificent wisteria had been trained to arch over the front door of the two-storey, two-bedroom dwelling, a smattering of crinkled amethyst blossoms still clinging on today amid the fresh emerald foliage; and a low hedge encircled the entire property, which included a well-stocked garden at the back. The gardeners from Leafley's tended to things here now, keeping the place in order.

As I stopped at the end of the path, a member of our usual cleaning team bustled out and headed for the van. I knew Shania well enough for her to call me Emmeline, though the upmarket agency frowned on first name terms.

It was the only large firm in the area, although I would have preferred handing money over to a cleaner directly rather than through the agency's owner, who was too snooty for my liking. But she paid a good wage and seemed to retain her staff, so what did I know? It wasn't as if I'd ever attempted running a business.

'What's going on?' I watched in confusion. 'What are you doing here?'

'Your guess is as good as mine, love.' She paused, hands on hips, her tabard apron pale blue, the company logo printed front and back. 'All I know is, Kay and I were meant to be off today, but we get asked if we can step in and blitz this place. Time and a half, and I didn't have firm plans, so I jumped at it. Same for Kay.'

'But...' Anything related to housekeeping was my department. I couldn't imagine my dad would have organised this. Least of all without running it past me. Or, more accurately, without getting me to do it for him. 'I don't understand.'

Shania shrugged. 'New tenant? A last minute arrangement, by the look of it.'

'A tenant?' I repeated, as if that might make things clearer; but it had the opposite effect.

I'd discussed renting out Donwell Cottage with my dad. It felt wrong to have it standing empty. He was nervous about any formal arrangements, though, and I hadn't been able to persuade him.

'It has to be a mistake. I never requested this.'

'As long as Kay and I get paid,' said Shania, doubt edging into her voice. 'But Mrs Augustine doesn't usually get things wrong. And the place needed a going-over, to be fair.'

It had been cleaned and aired when the last of our live-in employees moved out, and after draping the furniture in dust covers, I'd only stopped by to check on it now and again.

'Maybe ring the office?' Shania suggested cautiously. 'I'd best get on, though.' She lugged a caddy of cleaning products from the van.

I pulled out my phone and thumb-scrolled through my contacts. Mrs Augustine greeted me crisply and efficiently, and proceeded to answer my questions in the same manner. Apparently, it was my mother who'd phoned, not my father. Of course, aware of the marital situation, Mrs Augustine had rung Dad, to confirm the arrangement. But, once satisfied, she'd dispatched a cleaning crew forthwith. No expense spared.

'Why didn't you phone *me*, though?' I said, unable to disguise my annoyance.

'Your mother said not to bother you with this, Miss Midwynter, so I assumed...' She coughed delicately. 'I assumed you were indisposed. Your mother didn't actually say why she needed Donwell Cottage spick, span and sparkling, but I'll hazard a guess that it's about to be occupied at short notice.'

I let her ring off, wincing at the way she always seemed to drop the name of her firm into any conversation, as if she'd been so clever in coming up with it in the first place and liked to remind everyone, in case they'd dared forget.

A second later, I was ringing my mum.

'I didn't think you walked up that way very often,' was her first remark, as if that was the most important factor. 'I'm sorry, sweetheart. I didn't want to worry you.'

'Now I'm even more worried!'

'I'm sorry,' she said again, and sighed. 'It was all my idea, but until I knew for sure, I didn't want you to fret.'

'Mum, I'm fretting, okay? So you might as well tell me what's going on.'

'I think... to be honest... it's Jordi you should be speaking to. No one wanted to involve you yet, because... well, you have enough to deal with. I didn't think it fair to bring you into this until Jordi had decided one way or another. You only really needed to know if he agreed to the plan. Which, after some nagging on Deanna's part, he does. I mean, he's going along with it. And I'm sure he would have told you sooner rather than later.'

I shook my head in agitation, staring up at the cottage. What did this have to do with Jordi?

'He'll be at the school now,' I said, consulting my watch. 'I can't call him.'

'He won't be at school,' said my mother quietly. 'And I really don't want to say any more. It's his business, and it's up to him how he discloses it.'

'I'm not just anyone, though.'

'You know what I mean.'

'I don't, Mum. This is Jordi we're talking about—'

'Emmeline, please,' she cut in. 'Just try to get hold of him. He'll explain.' Her voice had acquired a flinty firmness now, signalling it was useless to argue. I recognised it well enough, though she rarely used it with me. But my mum wasn't one to take any nonsense, in spite of her natural warmth and empathy.

Flustered and cross, I gave in. 'Fine. Okay. Don't bother yourself, then.'

'I'll see you soon, Emmeline. Take care, sweetheart. And please... go easy on him.'

'On who?' I said obtusely. 'Dad? Or Jordi?'

'I suspect you're too soft with one and too hard on the other. Try to be more balanced. Jordi doesn't need any of your sass right now. He's not your brother. You both need to drop the old routine of antagonising each other for sport. You should have outgrown it years ago.'

'How do you even know what we're still like? And a while back you said you were glad he had me to talk to. I don't understand what's going on, because he obviously hasn't been talking to me about everything.'

'I'm still glad. And if I suspected the sniping between the two of you was anything other than a habit or an act, I wouldn't have made any suggestion to Deanna regarding Jordi's options. I would have left him where he was and just sympathised from afar. Now, I really am ending this call, before I say more than I should. I've probably gone too far already.'

'You haven't gone nearly far enough, Mum.'

But we mutually drew the conversation to a close. It was only going to lead to an argument I didn't have the stamina for.

Besides, truth be told, my fingers were itching to make another call.

Chapter 13

'Are you serious?'

Eyes wide, I stared at the man on my screen.

I'd FaceTimed him, needing to analyse his expressions, his tells. He hadn't answered initially, and I'd pounded up and down paths in agitation until he'd picked up, on my third attempt.

'Yeah,' he said now. 'Seems so. I'll be there at the weekend. Saturday afternoon, probably.'

He seemed a touch brighter than he'd looked recently. The scruffiness was still there, but he'd answered with a smile; I hadn't been able to rouse even a faint one the last time we'd spoken. A small one was preferable to none at all, but I became determined to coax more out of him, like a zealot on a mission. His misery could bring me down far lower than I wanted to go again. I wasn't about to stand idly by and let it triumph.

This all streamed through my head as I sat on a stone bench, watching him with narrowed eyes. He hummed and hawed and dragged his fingers through his hair, putting off the explanation I desperately needed to hear.

A short way away, ducks floated in blissful ignorance across a large ornamental pond, a willow dipping into the rippled, silky water. It was too tranquil a spot to hear bad news. Surely I wouldn't hear bad news. This ostentatious, but beautiful water feature hadn't been commissioned by my forebears as a tragic setting, a sad place. This was my favourite bench on the entire estate. Surely that wouldn't change now. Today.

'Jordi, are you ill?' I had to know, unable to bear the suspense any longer. 'Please just tell me. Is it... bad? Is it—'

'Shit, no.' He jerked upright in his chair. 'Is that what you've been thinking?'

'Only for the last twelve and a half minutes, since I spoke to my mum.'

'I'm so sorry. You've got a rampant imagination, Em.'

'If you'd heard her, Jordi... The way she made it sound, anyone might have jumped to the same conclusion. I take it you're not sick, then?'

'Not like that. Sick of the school. Sick of the bullshit I've been getting. Not sick of the kids. They're just stuck in a hopeless situation, and I only wish I could have done more. But it's the rest of it. The cronyism and elitism in the way its all managed now. And the minute I spoke up against it, I was labelled a shit-stirrer.'

'*What*? No way. What happened exactly?' I was so confused.

Relief washed over me, along with bewilderment. This wasn't as serious as my imagination had painted. At least in the sense that he wasn't ill; not in body. Perhaps too stressed and pale, but otherwise okay. It was a different sort of issue altogether, and I didn't understand. He was a great teacher, wasn't he? Deanna was proud of him. The kids all liked him. I couldn't fathom it. Jordi – fall foul of the administration? How, for pity's sake?

'It's an academy,' he said. 'The trust's owned by a mul-timillionaire and run like some all-powerful empire—'

'Very *Star Wars*.' I couldn't help myself.

'If you want to use that analogy, then I became a rebel. No lightsaber, though. No Jedi mind-powers. Just a bloke with a big mouth who didn't get on with the new head.'

'You got sacked?!'

'Let's just say it was mutual.'

'Oh, jeez. Jordi...' My insides crumpled in sympathy. Whatever he'd said or done, I couldn't believe the object of his disdain hadn't deserved it. He'd never been easily angered unless it was justified. Never swayed by fools. Jordi McAndrew Daley wouldn't bend simply because a stiff breeze blew in his direction.

'Look, I'm not panicking. There are plenty of schools with a different ethos. I'll find somewhere, but I don't have to rush into it. Mum's adamant I take my time and I know Dad would say the same, too...' Jordi looked away. 'Anyway, it is what it is. Your mum and mine think I need a change of scene, and they've dragged your dad into it. Poor sod never stood a chance, did he? So, that's what's happened. And they didn't think they should tell you from the start, because they didn't want you to worry, and possibly... regress or something.'

'Everyone's always treading on eggshells around me. Except you. I used to at least get plain honesty from you. Now, I'm not so sure.'

'You're hearing it from me, aren't you?'

'You're only telling me now because you have to; because apparently I'm going to have to put up with your smug-arse face in the flesh, and I won't be able to just hit a button and *poofff*, you're gone.'

He snorted. 'Nope. My smug-arse face will be right up in yours.'

'O-kay. That sounded weird.'

Now he was laughing, his cheeks tinged red, which made mine warm up, too, bizarrely. But he was laughing, praise be. I'd managed to make him laugh. Or it was a joint effort. Whatever.'

The laughter petered out. We grew serious again.

'I'll tell you more when I'm there,' he said. 'The ins and outs of it all. If you're fine listening to me drone on.'

'I'm always happy to listen. But Jordi... your mum? You've been helping her so much. Isn't she still relying on you? How can you get away? Is it because of your aunt? Your mum's sister.'

'Aunt Klara? What about her?'

'Is she coming over from New Zealand to stay with your mum for a while?'

'Er... no. Where did you get that idea from?'

'Oh. She got divorced last year, didn't she? I just thought she might come and help your mum out, support her a bit, you know.' I couldn't tell him the truth.

'No.' His brows had a baffled tilt to them now. 'Aunt Klara helps run some non-profit over there. She can't just swan off for a few weeks. Mum would hate it if she did; she'd feel too guilty.' Jordi wet his lips, hesitating. 'It's Matt, actually.'

'Matty?' I straightened on the bench.

'He's coming up to stay with Mum for a while.'

'Really? I thought you said he was too "flaky" to be relied on.'

'Well, I think he wants to prove me wrong. Or maybe

he's got his own stuff he needs to get away from, and isn't saying. Either way, Mum's happy he's coming, and just as insistent I take a break and get away.'

'Wow.'

Jordi seemed to be studying me closely, enough to make me squirm. 'You always put more faith in my brother than I did. Especially when you were *both* in London.'

'Did I?' Racking my brains, I tried to remember. I hadn't seen that much of him. Matty had been at a different uni. We'd only really started to bump into each other with increasing frequency later on, after Emma de Wynter came into being.

'He said you did.'

'Maybe I'd been drinking. And I can't say Matty ever returned the compliment.'

'Oh, he loved being associated with you. Wanted to bask in your glory.'

'Well, I never gave him any.' I frowned. 'Glory, I mean.'

Jordi blinked at me, looming rather close on my screen. 'If you say so. Matt's version might be different.'

'Version of what?' I was growing impatient of this. 'He's always thought I was weird and uncool, and if he changed his mind for a time, then everything that's happened since has probably changed it back again. But I'm glad,' I concluded.

'About what?'

'That he finally might be acting his age and not his shoe size. And that your mum's happy. Or happier. Or happy-ish—'

'Yeah. I get it. I just need her to stop fussing over me. That's the main reason I agreed to this plan.'

'So what are the other reasons, then?'

'To torment you *in person*, of course.'

'I'd expect no less.'

He paused – for effect, I think – before declaring, 'And to meet the infamous Miss Evans.'

I squealed, loud enough to startle a nearby duck. 'Oh, Jordi, really? Do you mean it? Because you're going to *love* her! She's the perfect woman for you...'

Considering the subject matter, his lips were spread in a rather grim line as I reeled off Polly's attributes.

Eventually, though, I reached the end of the list, and he managed to get a word in edgewise again.

'She better be as fabulous as you say she is, Em. Because it's going to take a hell of a lot to distract me.'

Chapter 14

I lay in bed that night finding sleep more elusive than ever. I hadn't been able to tell Jordi the truth; I knew by now how he'd react. But surely this new development was proof that my matchmaking abilities and my stories carried some credence.

It wasn't *exactly* how I'd written it, but then, there was no rule saying it had to be that precise. In the tale I was writing, his Aunt Klara – single again and rattling around her empty nest – had booked to come over to spend the summer in the UK with her sister. And Jordi, spurred on by his mum, who wouldn't need him so much with his aunt there, had asked if he could come to stay at the Hall for a couple of weeks in the school holidays.

It wasn't a bad place for a getaway. He'd spent some long weekends there over the years. Mostly when Dean and Deanna had come to visit, in happier days. I'd always tried my best to be around, too, so he didn't have to hang out with the 'oldies', as we used to call them, before we had more respect for the aging process.

So, it hadn't been too much of a stretch, having Jordi come to stay, especially as his holiday with Rosamunde had fallen through along with whatever future he'd been planning with her. And, as he would have earmarked a couple of weeks in his schedule for the trip – admittedly before his dad's more recent decline – he could have used that time to come to Shropshire instead.

Not quite Sardinia, but a welcome break, nevertheless.

This whole thing with the school had shocked me, though. I hadn't seen it coming. And I hadn't counted for Jordi's mental health in my story, beyond his break-up and the ongoing pressure with his parents. I had to concede it might not be the best time for him to embark on a new relationship. But if it was going to be with anyone, there was nobody better than Polly.

Having Jordi turn up at Midwynter Hall sooner than I'd written would also fit better with the whole Zac situation. With Jordi around, Polly would soon see I'd been right. He was a much worthier match than Zachary Martin. And the fact my parents had decided to install him in the cottage was inspired.

I wondered if Mum had told Dad about my plans for Jordi and Polly, and if Dad had subsequently convinced her I knew what I was doing. I rarely got anything wrong in his eyes. But having Jordi staying in his own private space would be more discreet than up at the Hall. It could provide him with the ideal backdrop to romance Polly. More than Zac seemed able to offer, stuck with his mum and sisters, probably because he couldn't afford to move out.

I could see Donwell Cottage now on a summer evening, the little bistro table and chairs in the garden, gently illuminated by candles in jars hanging from the two fine plum trees; wine flowing and music playing. Jordi, even more Hemsworthy than usual, in an open-necked shirt, reaching across the table to take Polly's hand before leading her indoors...

Mmm. Very nice. The perfect evening. So perfect in fact, that it was making me rather hot. I kicked off the duvet. Maybe I ought to jot some of this down. Carry on with the story. There was living vicariously, however, and there was knowing when to close the bedroom door and keep my beak out of their business. I wasn't going to write about that aspect of things.

For all I knew – and now I was sitting up in bed, frowning – Jordi was lacking in that department. Not in terms of equipment; I'd been unfortunate enough to have walked in on him once in a wetroom, many years ago; mortifying us both, until we learned to laugh about it.

But perhaps in the sense that a woman needed someone skilful and sensitive to her needs, and Jordi might never have learned the art of lovemaking to any leg-trembling degree.

Was that why girlfriends dumped him, rather than the other way around? Because he didn't deliver? Surely they could have given him a little guidance? It wasn't a one-way street.

But this really wasn't something I cared to dwell on when dealing with real-life people, especially when I knew these two so well.

It had been fine having my fictional couples getting up to all sorts in my books. I'd just let my imagination run wild back then.

My readers understood that, didn't they? There were few lovers who were that swoonworthy and attentive in reality, and no one expected an actual living person to act that heroic, or be that considerate and accomplished in every aspect of the process – from the first tentative sparks to the full-on fireworks.

I wondered, not for the first time, whether readers thought Emma de Wynter had been more experienced than she really was. Whether they assumed she'd had a string of passionate affairs, and wrote about love with such expertise because she knew all there was to know.

From the depths of despair to the dopamine-induced highs.

Very few people believed that was true, surely? I'd made it clear I'd dated a few damp squibs in my time? Known my share of (mild) heartache? My ego bruised, but only for a moment, before picking myself up off the sofa, putting the ice cream back in the freezer and the wine in the fridge, and getting on with my life as if I hadn't just had a boyfriend cheat on me?

No one I'd dated had ever merited the trauma of a thoroughly broken heart. And I'd aspired to empower women to realise their self-worth, to resist having it snatched away by an incompetent, selfish lover. I'd wanted Emma de Wynter to show her vulnerabilities as well as her strengths, and I'd achieved all that... hadn't I?

Actually, I couldn't measure what I'd achieved by the end. Sadly, I'd had to stop interacting with true fans (as well as the trolls) due to the sheer overwhelm of their adoration. The intensity of their feelings. Their need to tell me about every awful thing that had happened to them, and how I'd given them hope, when all I'd done was make up wild plots about people who didn't exist.

Sitting at the desk in my bedroom now, bare toes digging in the soft pile of the carpet, I stared at the cursor blinking on my screen. I'd got as far as Jordi arriving at

Midwynter Hall, though I hadn't written the meet-cute yet. It had to be just right. A simple introduction was boring. The expectations would be running high, and I had to present them both in their best light.

One step at a time.

Polly would be looking as pretty as she always did. I'd never known her look otherwise, even with varying degrees of bloom in her cheeks. It was Jordi, and his present state of disarray, that needed addressing.

My fingers poised to type, I pictured how he could look at his best; how I'd *seen* him look with my own eyes. I had to acknowledge, the man was more than half-decent. And when he matched his manners to his appearance, he was probably charming in every respect.

It had no effect on me because, well, he was just Jordi, and I'd known him in his dorky teenage years and his slightly less dorky twenties. I'd heard him burp. I'd caught him picking his spots. I'd seen him uncharacteristically inebriated after a night out once, babbling about true love being an "f-ing lie"; not a pleasant experience trying to bundle all six-foot-one of him into a taxi on my own.

Plus, he'd never turned his charm on me. Quite the opposite. I got the dregs. Jordi at his worst; or his most human. And expecting the same of me. Not that I was good at it.

But to start with, making the most of that all too influential first impression, Polly needed to see the prime behind the grime.

Criminal. I blew out air through my nostrils. *If you keep coming out with stuff like that, you don't deserve to be published ever again.*

Besides, even though I hadn't been able to sniff him, I didn't doubt Jordi was showering regularly. He couldn't be grimy, as such.

Still. Polly needed to see his full potential.

In short, she had to see in him what I *didn't* see.

Chapter 15

The weekend was upon us, and I stood in Donwell Cottage, hands on hips, assessing my handiwork with pride and one last critical gaze, seeking out any imperfection I could quickly put right. Thanks to next day delivery options at online check-outs, I'd transformed the cottage from an older man's home of thirty odd years into a younger man's cosy, yet masculine and upmarket, bachelor pad. Definitely not the sort that might imply women weren't welcome during daylight hours.

From monochrome tartan cushions on the sofa downstairs, to matching duvet in the main bedroom. A well-stocked larder and fridge packed with nutritious essentials, alongside Malbec and Pinot Noir in the wine rack. Paracetamol and a box of precautions stowed away in the bathroom cabinet. Honey and black pepper hand-made soap bars; a stack of plump, charcoal grey towels; and air freshener spray – the sort that didn't make me cough – in a crisp linen scent.

In the garden, I'd decided candles in jars were impractical, so opted for solar-powered bulbs strung like bunting around the small patio, quaintly rustic with its large slabs of rough-hewn stone and terracotta pots full of scented, feathery herbs. The garden borders were just tidy enough, and beginning to pop with colour.

All in all, the little accents I'd indulged in were justified by my reasoning that Jordi ought to feel comfortable, and at home on the estate, for as long as he wanted. It wasn't solely about putting Polly at ease by making his presence here seem less of a transitory thing, or even setting the right mood for amorous encounters. I needed Jordi to think of Donwell Cottage as a haven, the way I thought of the Hall itself.

My phone pinged.

> —Delayed by traffic. Got hungry so stopped at some services. Just make sure there's a key in the box safe thing you gave me the code to. Don't wait around, no idea how long I'll be.

As if I *wouldn't* wait. Or had better things to do.

Dad was on the golf course with his regular buddies from the club, and I'd already made rocky road mini bites early that morning to give them plenty of time to set, remembering they were Jordi's favourite, particularly the variety his mum had perfected. I'd emailed Deanna for the recipe. Not being keen on them myself, and knowing Dad wasn't either, I'd never bothered to attempt them before.

Our former groundskeeper had fitted a key-safe, in case he ever locked himself out, or for cleaners to let themselves in, and I'd mentioned it to Jordi in my numerous messages over the last couple of days. I'd felt the need to clarify what he did or didn't have to bring with him, what basics I'd ordered food-wise, how the Wi-Fi would be back up and running as soon as possible; in short, everything I deemed significant enough to point out ahead of his arrival.

His final response, when I'd exhausted myself, had been brief.

> — You didn't need to go to so much trouble. But thank you.

And at that point I'd run out of words, because I didn't know how to go about explaining. I wanted him there for my own selfish reasons. It would be fun to have him around, winding me up, making me laugh, introducing him to Polly: another of my favourite people.

However, putting him up at the cottage also meant I could easily slip away once I'd reached the end of my tether with his baiting. It was refreshing that he never tried to smother me in bubble-wrap, but even that had its limits. When I'd had enough, I could make my excuses and slip away.

Mum had asked me to tone down the sass, and presumably that meant the sarcasm, too, but I wasn't certain how to interact with Jordi without it, and I had a hunch he'd feel the same. There was much more to it than whatever was on the surface. It was a language all our own. But fine, if she wanted 'balance', I would give it a go and be mild-tempered and sympathetic and *nice* a bit more often in his company, although I suspected we'd both get bored of it and revert to our usual ways.

I sank on to the sofa, picking up one of the books I'd brought over from the library at the Hall. I'd thought a selection of carefully curated first editions might interest Jordi; though not the oldest or most valuable, which had to remain behind glass. So I'd made a neat and tempting stack on the coffee table.

Unfortunately, a good night's sleep had eluded me again yesterday, and my eyelids were soon fluttering heavily. With a yawn, I put the book aside. A short nap might help. I would wake up energised, bright and breezy, and in the best mood to welcome Jordi and listen to his misfortunes in greater detail. I was desperate to hear more. He could unburden himself without any censure from me.

The next thing I knew, though, a soft weight was being draped over my legs, and for a moment I gave into it, wriggling to get more comfortable, mumbling to myself until I heard a quiet chuckle.

I tried to sit upright, but weighed down with sleep it was nothing better than a drunken-style lurch.

'Wah?!' came out of my mouth, possibly with a tiny bit of dribble.

'Not sure that's a word.'

I fought to open my gummy eyes, wiping my mouth with the back of my hand. Slowly, I realised the grey throw I'd bought to match the cushions was spread across my lap. Someone was standing near me. They smelled sandalwoody and musky and pleasant, and seemed to be leafing through a book.

'Are these all first editions?'

'Jordi?' I blinked rapidly, my limbs still sluggish as I tried to move.

'Hi, Em.' There was a smile in his voice. 'I didn't mean to wake you. You looked really peaceful.'

'Jordi!' I scrambled clumsily to my feet, pushing aside the throw. Overwhelmed by a rush of delight, and relief that he'd arrived safely – though I hadn't noticed earlier that I was worrying – I threw myself at him.

It was an attempt at a hug, but he didn't seem to know how to respond.

'Whoa,' he muttered, and pushed me away. 'Since when were you a hugger?'

'Always.' But I sounded doubtful, and prodded at my memory, trying to establish what I'd done in the past where the McAndrew Daley brothers were concerned.

'We never hug. It's not our thing.'

'I'm pretty sure I remember doing it with Matty.' But I still sounded dubious, and scratched my head, as if that might trigger confirmation that if I'd hugged one brother I must have hugged the other.

'He wasn't that memorable, then.' Jordi stepped back further.

I swayed there, discombobulated, taking him in. The solid mass of him. He was actually here! Not just on a screen. And quite normal for him, he was frowning at me. I shouldn't be surprised or upset.

'Well, hello, and happy to see you, too,' I said at last, darkly and with a strange bruised passion; mortified by his reaction.

Whether or not we'd ever hugged shouldn't matter. I'd been glad to see him, and we were grown-ups, for pity's sake. Maybe my mum had been right. We needed to move past the awkward and antagonistic phase we seemed to have got stuck in. We had to face up to who we'd become, not act like the adolescents we once were.

He stood studying me so inscrutably, I wondered if he could read my thoughts and was cautiously taking the measure of them. 'Sorry,' he mumbled at last. 'It was a rubbish journey.'

'That's ok,' I mumbled back.

He shook his head vehemently. 'It's not. Because it's good to be here. And I owe you—'

'No. No, you don't. This wasn't even my idea, Jordi. All I've done is...' I glanced around and had to stop. I'd actually done a lot, once I'd known what was going on. I hadn't hidden it in my messages, and I couldn't pretend otherwise now. It was more than obvious. Perhaps Jordi had already been poking around in the fridge with raised eyebrows.

Suddenly, the idea of him rummaging through the bathroom cabinet and seeing *everything* I'd ordered on his behalf, made me cringe. Had I gone too far? For Polly's sake, I hadn't wanted to leave anything to chance.

'Financially, I owe you, Em. Even if you don't want my

thanks for everything else.'

'I didn't spend much,' I lied, knowing I hadn't reined in the purse strings.

'I'll pay you back.'

'The hell you will, Jordi. You're not just our guest, you're family. Dad and I want you to feel at home here, and you're welcome for as long as you like.'

His eyes dodged mine, staring off to the side. I took advantage and raked my gaze over him in his entirety, rather than just the top half I'd viewed on a screen the last few years.

In dark jeans and a casual checked shirt, sleeves rolled up to the elbows, he was looking healthier than I'd seen him of late, though healthy meant different things to different people and Polly's assessment might not match mine. Zac, for instance, was a bit rangy for my liking. Anyway, Jordi had neatened his stubble and trimmed his hair since we'd last spoken, so the unkemptness was gone. Just as I'd written in my story.

Polly wouldn't be immune, surely. I recalled how she'd thought her friend's bloke in the village was fanciable, and in terms of build, Jordi wasn't too different. He was fair, though, and his hair only had kinks in it rather than curls. Still Thor-like, to some degree, although not as shaggy.

'There's moussaka for your dinner tonight,' I went on.

'I made extra yesterday when I cooked for Dad and myself so there'd be a portion left over for you. You used to like that, didn't you? You only need to heat it up. I didn't think you'd feel like cooking today, or be up for supper at the Hall. But I bought three steaks for tomorrow. You can handle those, I assume, or do you need my help?'

He looked at me again, his brow creased. 'What's tomorrow?'

I wavered, but then launched right in. He'd asked for an introduction, and I was only fulfilling his request. 'Meeting Polly. I've asked her over for dinner here, at the cottage. The three of us. Her mum's dropping her off, but I thought you might drive her home afterwards? Pebblestow's not far, and it'll give you a chance to talk alone, get to know each other.'

He nodded slowly. 'Sounds good, I guess.'

'Oh, come on, Jordi. A bit more enthusiasm, please. She's an amazing person.'

'Why don't you go out with her, then?' he bit back. Not as keen as he'd seemed a matter of days ago, which narked me. I frowned at his ingratitude. I'd gone to all this trouble; I wasn't about to have it thrown back in my face.

'If I was that way inclined, I might. Although I don't think women are her preference, either.'

'So, I'm definitely her type, just by way of being a bloke?'

'Well, I know for a fact you have a dick as well as acting like one,' I snapped. 'So I'd say, yes – you're more her cup of tea.'

Jordi's eyes widened but he let out a short, hoarse laugh, redolent of a sea lion, while I felt myself blush again, having alluded to that walking-in-on-him-in-the-wetroom incident, even though it was aeons ago.

'Talking of tea,' he said, 'I'm gagging for one, actually. And you know, Em, you can act like a dick, too.'

'Takes one to know one.' It was a naff retort. Ruffled and hot, I stalked off to boil the kettle, though that was as far as I was prepared to go; he could make a brew for the both of us. He was right behind me, so I added with a hiss, 'You always bring out the worst in me. I don't know why I delude myself otherwise. The mugs are in that cupboard, by the way.'

He didn't deign to respond, but took out two mugs and set them on the worktop.

As I watched him make the tea, I apologised to my lovely mother in my head; but really, she should have been aware this was a hopeless case.

Throwing in the metaphorical towel, I accepted what I'd already known deep down. Alone or with company, when Jordi and I were together, we were never going to behave like adults.

Chapter 16

I put up with Jordi that afternoon long enough to watch him tuck into the rocky road mini bites, while we had two mugs of tea each, and discussed the creative writing course and his assignments and ideas, while shying away from the heavier issues lurking like two elephants in the room (at least they could keep each other company).

Jordi was too tired from his journey to go into everything that had happened over the last month or so. Save it, he said, for when he was in a better mood. I couldn't complain because I didn't want to talk about my agoraphobia, either, though I knew I couldn't be evasive indefinitely. It would be far more obvious to Jordi while he was here than when he'd been all those miles away, and eventually it would be impossible to avoid the subject.

'It'll be weird at the next session,' I said, referring to his online course, 'knowing you're only over here when we're all logged on.'

He'd postponed it last week, citing personal issues,

which had sent the WhatsApp group into a frenzy of speculation. I'd felt superior; party to information I knew I couldn't share, yet at the same time protective of Jordi and perturbed by a few of the digs, namely from Frankie. I hadn't contributed beyond *I'm sure he'll be fine for next week*, because I hadn't wanted to draw too much attention to myself.

In her typical fashion, Hetty had written several paragraphs about how wonderful Jordi was, how he'd helped her so much with her writing, and how far she'd come. She wasn't about to begrudge him a week off. He was such a gentleman, so encouraging, so gallant. Even when he was doling out constructive criticism, he never made her feel as if she'd failed. Jordi always said what she *needed* to hear to keep her motivated, and she'd started sharing her stories with her mother, because he'd given her the confidence to do so, and truly, they were quite long stories, and her mother was very patient in agreeing to listen.

No surprise, it went on a bit. I'd also skim-read Nancy-Jane's reaction, noting she was more subdued than other times. In the end, it was Cole who'd calmed the frenzy and put it all into context. I'd inwardly agreed that everyone was being OTT, but I'd been too wary to say it. Cole had framed it better than I could. He was probably the most talented out of all of us and the least likely to turn anything into a drama, bar a short story of his he was reworking as a screenplay.

I'd simply been glad I had more time to work on the latest assignment, considering I'd put it aside to focus on Jordi and Polly's 'romantasy', as I'd started describing my tales. Strictly speaking, they were only fantasy because they hadn't happened yet, and nothing to do with the fusion of genres that seemed to be firing Hetty's imagination, judging by her offering at one of our recent sessions.

'You can be honest, you know,' said Jordi, when I eventually took my leave.

I needed to get back to Dad, who'd already sent me a few concerned texts. I'd negligently not been waiting when he got back from golf, ready and eager to ask how he'd got on.

'Honest?' I said. 'About what?'

'The course. If you're finding it helpful. I want to discuss your writing in depth now that I'm here. You're getting talked about more and more in book circles. Are you aware?'

I shrugged, trying to look nonchalant even though, in truth, it daunted me. 'I think Nancy-Jane and the others can't work out what I'm doing among them. I feel like an interloper wherever I am.'

'Except here.' Standing at the cottage door, Jordi gestured to our surroundings. 'You're at home here.'

I looked around, compelled to nod. 'I always have been.'

'And there's safety in that.'

My gaze met his, before darting away. 'I suppose.' I could tell where this was heading, but it wasn't the time to discuss a possible life beyond Midwynter Hall.

I steered it back to 'work'.

'Imposter syndrome is real and thriving when it comes to my career,' I confided. 'I mean, I can't even call it a "career" without wanting to laugh. Every time I get royalties, I can't believe what I'm seeing; even now, after all this time. None of it seems to have anything to do with me any more. I just get Dad's accountant to invest it for me, but somewhere it can do some good, make a difference.'

I twitched in discomfort, sensing Jordi's gaze, warm and approving. 'Don't look at me like that,' I added. 'I'd be sacrificing a lot more if I was a really good person. My life's cushy here, but I'm not ashamed. I'm... relieved.'

'At least you're honest,' said Jordi, after a pause. 'Conscious of some things, if not others.'

I should have stopped there, but I found myself saying, 'Why would I want to disturb the status quo?'

'Because,' he said softly, 'there's a lot you're missing out on.'

'Well... I don't like to be greedy.'

'So you're not planning to ever have another relationship, then?'

'Another?' I laughed. 'I'm not sure I've ever had *one*, Jordi. I've had "ships", I admit, but not the sort you're talking about, lasting months rather than just weeks. Unlike you.'

'Me?' His turn to laugh grimly. 'I think you've overestimated my "ships", too. Apparently I'm like Teflon after a while. Nothing and no one sticks. Never to do with them, it seems. The blame's all mine. At least I'm consistent. It's not that I don't try, but... I probably bore them into breaking up with me.'

'Is that what they've told you?'

They were all fools if they thought they could do better.

Jordi was never boring. Irksome as hell, but never dull.

'It's what I know.' He sighed, and shook his head. 'Anyway, you'd better go, before your dad texts you again. Tell him I'll come up tomorrow during the day to say hi.'

'Leave it till Monday. Mum and Randall won't be over tomorrow; there's some comp or tournament on, and

Dad'll be at the club all day. I'll make him some supper he can warm up, before I come over here. I want to arrive before Polly.'

'So efficient.'

'Of course. I need to be around for the meet-cute. Can't miss that.'

'Naturally.' His mouth set into a hard line.

Strolling back up to the Hall, I hummed to myself, trying not to be fazed. If everything worked out like my story, Jordi would be smiling again before too long.

Chapter 17

Polly had stopped answering my messages around lunchtime.

I had a feeling I'd exasperated her; interrogating her on her choice of attire for that evening, checking she was still okay with Jordi taking her home, making sure she knew her mum just had to drop her at the gates and not waste time driving all the way up to the main house. But I so badly wanted the night to go without a hitch.

I'd given up trying to get an answer out of my friend, though, and had conceded she might not *be* my friend for much longer if I didn't just ease off.

I was back at Donwell Cottage at six-thirty on the dot, pleased to find Jordi had prepped the veg, and the steaks were out of the fridge, to be cooked last minute.

'You look… nice,' said Jordi, as I inspected his efforts in the kitchen.

'Oh.' I glanced down at my broderie anglaise maxi dress. 'Thank you. It's old, though.'

'It's pretty.'

I shot him a frown. 'Don't forget to compliment Polly, too. I'm sure she'll make an extra-special effort, and a woman likes to know her time's been well spent.'

'If you say so. Your hair's amazing these days. It looked good long, but it suits you more in that bob. I don't think I've ever told you that.'

'Er, thank-you?' I shifted from one foot to the other, tucking a strand of the admired hair behind my ear, an unwelcome warmth creeping up my neck. 'You look good, too,' I added, for want of something to say, and because it was courteous to return the compliment.

'You reckon? This shirt's not too much?'

It was a dark twilight shade, accentuating the sandy streaks in his hair and the blue of his eyes, his light gold forearms standing out against the rolled-up shirtsleeves.

A far cry from the pasty, lanky boy I'd first met all those years ago. But then, I wasn't a little girl with jelly sandals and a million glittery clips in my hair, following him and Matty around like a shadow that first summer. Before I'd been disillusioned, and realised for the most part that boys were indeed made of slugs and snails, like the version of the nursery rhyme I knew best, though the puppy-dogs' tails sounded too nice to be applied to them.

'Er, no.' I pulled my gaze away. 'Not too much. Just

right, I think.'

'I put some Malbec to chill. It feels too warm to serve it at room temp. I'll only have a small glass, seeing as I'm driving later.'

I absently concurred, then checked my watch. 'Polly should be here soon.'

After a weird and angsty silence, Jordi gestured to the patio. 'Do you think it's warm enough to eat outside?'

He followed me through the door. The air, scented with honeysuckle, felt soft against my skin, but suddenly I was conscious of my bare shoulders, the straps of my dress rather narrow, and I went inside for my denim jacket.

'Too cold?'

'No,' I muttered, stepping back out again. 'I mean, I don't know. It might be pleasant to eat alfresco, but we'll see what Polly says.' I plonked myself down on one of the chairs. 'Did you have a productive day?'

Jordi settled opposite. 'If you can call unpacking productive?'

'Making yourself at home, finding space for things – it's important.'

'Yeah.' He scratched his temple. 'It's generous of your dad, letting me stay rent-free.'

His voice was sombre, which wasn't setting the right tone. I couldn't have him maudlin when Polly arrived or before we'd even drunk a drop of the wine.

'Honestly, it's no problem. The cottage was empty. We're still deciding what to do with it. I suppose we could get a new groundsman, but I've taken over organising that side of things.'

'I can see how that suits your... domineering nature. But you don't do the DIY and maintenance, too?'

'Not when you put it like that, no. A bit of painting and weed-pulling – but I farm out the bulk of the work to local firms. There's no live-in staff here these days.'

'A massive contrast to how Midwynter Hall would have been run years ago.'

'A world away. I'm housekeeper and cook, for a start, so I keep the keys to my own spice cupboard. And I do the laundry, too. But all of that's fine, because I prefer being busy. Thankfully we have cleaners who come in regularly – I couldn't have coped with that alone. I've never been a fan of scrubbing toilets.'

'Don't know anyone who is.'

'You'd be surprised. There's an art to it. And YouTube videos.'

'But there's a big difference between maintaining a property the size of the Hall, and a three-bed semi, for instance.'

'True. I remember trying to keep my flat tidy. Let's just

say I'm better at the domestic stuff than I used to be.' I picked at my nails even though I'd taken the time to file and paint them earlier in the day and was jeopardising my own handiwork. 'But I still feel I ought to do things differently. Around here, I mean. I'd like to be more... enterprising. Put some of the space to better use. I'm not sure how much Dad would go for it, though. He's become more set in his ways.'

'If anyone can cajole him, it's you.'

I met Jordi's gaze, but again, for whatever reason, I couldn't hold it for long. My excitement at having him around seemed to have mutated into unease, as if it had been so long since I'd been in his company in a non-virtual sense, I'd forgotten how to go about it.

'I think you're overestimating my influence. My dad thinks I'm perfect, but that doesn't mean I have perfect ideas or schemes when it comes to this place.'

'So – these ideas – do you have anything specific in mind, or are they still vague?'

'I—' The sound of an enthusiastic car horn startled me. It shattered the tranquillity, and seemed to shatter something else, as well – a bubble around the garden I couldn't quite define, blocking out everything beyond Jordi and me and our conversation at the little wrought iron table. 'That must be Polly.' Although her mum had never tooted like that.

Jordi sprang to his feet. He looked eager, boding well for the evening. I rose, too, and followed him around the side of the house, along a shingled path inset with circular stones and flanked by fragrant shrubs. I couldn't have penned a lovelier setting, although I'd bashed out a decent effort on my laptop.

But the sight that greeted us by the main gates definitely *wasn't* the pivotal scene I'd pictured only days earlier.

Chapter 18

'Hey!' Polly was scrambling out of a small, low-slung convertible.

It was old, even I could see that, although I knew very little about cars. And it wasn't her mother in the driving seat.

I scowled at the man behind the wheel. But I might have just looked as if I was squinting into the sun as it dipped towards the horizon, because he responded with a grin and a wave.

Polly was in jeans and a plain T-shirt, hair tousled, face blotchy and shiny. It hardly made the best first impression. She hooked her backpack over her shoulder, and beamed at Zachary Martin.

'Thanks for a great afternoon. And for dropping me off.'

'No problem. I had a great time, too.'

Jordi, who seemed more interested in the car than the young woman who'd alighted from it, gave my friend a nod, then leaned towards Zac. 'She's a beauty.'

Polly winked, and bounded in my direction. 'Hard to believe, but they don't mean yours truly!' As she hugged me, I flinched at her clamminess. 'Sorry, Em,' she gabbled, 'you look *amazing*, and I did intend to go home first to shower and change. We went for a walk, or a hike or whatever, in the hills, and it took longer than we thought. I know I look a state.'

'Do you have any make-up in that bag? And body spray?' I whispered imperiously, steeling myself for the trademark eye roll.

'I'll do my best to make myself presentable, ma'am. Just point me to the bathroom.'

'Jordi,' I called to him, in a brittle fashion, 'I'll be inside with Polly.'

He pulled himself away from the car long enough to glance in our direction. 'I'm sorry, I'll be a better host in a minute, I swear.'

You'd better be. I included him in a fresh scowl, before marching Polly indoors. I'd never realised Jordi was such a car geek, and I apologised to Polly as I steered her to the bathroom.

'It's a classic,' she explained, through the door, as I waited outside. 'The car.'

'I guessed that.'

'Zac did it up, *fixed* it up, whatever you call it. Bought it at an auction. It's his baby. He's cleverer than he makes out. Knows a lot about mechanics; and gardening, of course.'

'You mean, he knows how to use a ride-on mower?'

'Not just that. He's really into nature. Kept pointing things out on our walk, and—'

'I can't imagine his car's that low on fuel emissions. Which is a bit hypocritical, to me.'

'I didn't say he was perfect.' Her voice had hardened. 'He doesn't use it that much. I think he bought it with his dad's help.'

'He has a dad, then? I thought he lived with his mum and sisters.'

'His parents aren't together. And his sisters are half-sisters. But apparently his dad's local, too. There aren't any other siblings.'

She knew so much, already. Zac was either an over-sharer, or he liked her a lot. I suspected the latter, though both might be true.

I speculated how he could have afforded a car like that, but if he'd done it up himself, maybe it hadn't been such a financial stretch, and it might have been cheap to begin with. Being the opposite of an expert in that field, I had no notion of how much it might cost to maintain and insure, alongside all the other expenses.

'Jordi's manners can be a lot better than this.' I peered through the small window at the end of the landing.

Down below, both men were still deep in conversation, poring over the engine now.

The irony of it! The audacity. Although who exactly was being audacious probably depended on the viewpoint. Did Zac know I was setting Jordi up with Polly? Was he aware Jordi was a rival?

Polly finally emerged from the bathroom, enveloped in a floral scent that was less likely to offend; her skin a perfect balance between matte and dewy. 'Thank goodness for freshening wipes! Plastic-free and biodegradable, of course, before you set the eco-police on me.'

'You've sprayed yourself, too?' I checked.

'And powdered my nose. I'm not a slut, Em. Well, not that sort.'

'What sort?'

'Not the sort you mustn't shame me for.'

'What...?' I intensified my scowl. 'You're being like this on purpose. You know I wanted this evening to go without a hitch—'

Cutting through my frustration, Jordi called up the stairs at last, and I chivvied Polly along the landing, definitely not in the mood for games, riddles, or taunting.

If neither of them could muster a scrap of gratitude for my efforts, they could at least be on their best behaviour. Although, I didn't actually need a thank you. I only wanted a pleasant evening to showcase them at their finest.

It hadn't started well.

'Seems like a good bloke,' said Jordi, as we came downstairs. 'Knows his stuff.'

'He does, doesn't he?' Polly grinned at him. 'Pleased to meet you officially. As you've probably already gathered, I'm—'

'Polly. I know.' Jordi grinned back. 'I've heard a lot about you. All good, before you ask.'

'Same. In fact, I'd go as far as to say what I've heard is excellent.'

I stood back, resisting the urge to rub my hands together.

Okay. Things might be looking up, after all.

'You're exaggerating, surely.' Jordi addressed Polly, before offering me a quizzical, teasing look. 'Em doesn't think that highly of me.'

'I think you're *both* fabulous when you put your minds to it,' I answered quickly. 'Which doesn't happen that often, in your case.' I shot him a withering glance. 'But enough so that I can introduce you to each other with no qualms.'

'See?' said Polly. 'When it comes to you, she's qualmless.'

'High praise indeed,' Jordi agreed. And they shared a look that was more than I could have hoped for at this early stage.

Which was when the Strange Thing happened.

I felt – though only for a moment, before I managed to fight back – excluded and lonely, and on the outside of something.

In essence, *not* happy.

Even less happy than when Polly had arrived with Zac, and I'd wondered if she'd done it deliberately to ruffle me, considering she had a rebellious streak and every now and again she put her foot down with a giant stomp.

'Right,' I said, too brightly perhaps, to mask my confusion, 'Jordi, could you please sort us out with drinks?'

For someone who had just been on a date with one man, Polly was doing an astonishing job at expressing her interest in another. Almost brazen in its extravagance; I barely recognised her.

She seemed to know exactly what to say and do to put Jordi at ease and register the fact she found him fascinating. And not solely in a lascivious way, as she had with Zac when they'd first met, but on an intellectual level, which left me a touch confounded. It didn't seem to be just about having 'a bit of fun', then, but the start of something deeper and more meaningful.

Only... she'd claimed she didn't want that.

Hadn't she?

Or had I been right not to be convinced?

Because here she was, devoting all her attention to Jordi as if her eggs were suddenly all in one basket and she was perfectly happy to have them there, everyone else forgotten in the haze of whatever it was she was feeling right now.

But more importantly, why should it unsettle me so much, anyway, when I'd declared all along they could be perfect together? I ought to be jubilant, and smugly braying, *I told you so.*

As the evening went on, she even managed to get him talking about the events which had led up to him leaving his job, and I sat back and listened without interrupting. It seemed a private conversation between two people who had only just met but clearly shared a reciprocal attraction, or a vision of what-might-be. Something I might never understand.

And perhaps that was the problem. The fact that so

many aspects of my stories had to be imagined, although I wasn't even producing science fiction.

I had to *pretend* I understood what I was writing about.

When I wrote about passion, I was never remembering how I'd felt around a person. It was simply a heady concentration distilled from my love of wielding words and my adoration of Midwynter Hall.

So... possibly... I was jealous. Jealous of whatever they might share one day. Jealous that I'd never felt it myself in a romantic setting. The famed lightning bolt realisation. That connection which screams out of nowhere.

It's You. Here You Are. I Thought I'd Never Find You. Stuff to that effect, at least.

I wasn't so much a fly rubbing its hand-like limbs together with what seemed to be diabolical glee, but a fly on the wall not doing very much of anything, as I listened to a conversation I wanted to be a part of, yet unable to breach whatever it was they'd erected around themselves.

'You're uncharacteristically quiet,' Jordi said eventually, as if he'd just noticed me sitting there, playing with my wine glass.

'Am I?' Silly response, because I knew his observation was true. 'There's just a lot to digest. The official line for you quitting so unexpectedly is stress; though they're not adding who caused that stress, are they?' I shook my head, sickened by the way his superiors had handled the situation. 'I still remember why you got into teaching in the first place. Or one of the reasons. You said there were some kids who saw school as their safe space, somewhere they could escape whatever was going on at home. You had a friend, you said, whose dad was violent...'

Jordi's eyebrows pinched, as he drifted into the past, I assumed, where I'd sent him. 'I thought I could help. But now I see kids in school who don't feel heard or safe there, either. I'm not the only one who thinks the current model needs an overhaul. As it stands, it's just one giant exam factory, except you always have a certain proportion who fail. And we're being too slow about preparing them for real life. The kids I taught might have known all there was to know about single celled organisms, but not enough about how to deal with things like budgeting and bills, or mortgages and tax. That all seemed too rushed, to me. Too haphazard. In my school, at any rate.'

'I'm not sure even the taxman knows everything there is to know about tax,' said Polly.

'Probably not. Anyway,' he sighed, 'all I seem to have been doing, is either teaching them how to ace exams, or scrape a pass at best. And don't get me started on the kids who are off-rolled just so they don't negatively impact a school's "ratings".'

'Have you thought about teaching primary?' Polly piped up again.

I grumbled to myself. She'd beaten me to the question.

'I've considered it. *Am* considering it.' Jordi shrugged. 'It's a myth that it's easier just because the kids are younger, though. Not as simple a leap as it sounds.'

'What about the writing course?' I said. 'Couldn't you develop that into something with a broader scope? Wasn't that your plan, anyway?'

'It still is, but I need a more conventional job alongside it, at least at this stage. I'm also working on another course, which wouldn't be live; for passive income. Something people could download at their leisure. And maybe short, intensive workshops I can open for a few days at a time, two or three times a year, with more participants. But none of that happens overnight. And the market's already crowded.'

'You still aim to focus on writers who can't easily access in-person courses, though?' This was how he'd lured me into his scheme in the first place – eager as well as anxious for my opinion.

His gaze met mine, as determined as ever. 'Absolutely. I want them to have the same opportunities for mentoring and coaching as anyone else.'

'Levelling the playing field,' said Polly.

I sniffed. 'Don't be too keen to "other us", Jordi. It's all very admirable, but you come off as patronising sometimes.'

'On the course?!' He instantly looked concerned. 'Has anyone said anything to you – privately, I mean?'

I'd got myself into a bit of a pickle here when all I'd been aiming for was a share of the conversation. The last thing I wanted was to wound Jordi's feelings or dent his confidence.

'Um... if it's private, I can't actually say, can I? You have fans,' I went on carefully, 'but one or two of the others – well, maybe just one – might not exactly—'

'Frankie.' His expression grew stern. 'Frankie doesn't look favourably on me, I know. And off the record, Em, the same holds true in reverse.'

'Oh?' There'd been a hint of tension lately, but... 'You can be so impartial, though. When it comes to our work.'

'The man's paying me for a service. I make an effort to treat him the same as everyone else. And, look, I know you have a soft spot for him, so I'm not going to put you in an awkward position. Let's just leave it.'

'Me?' I spluttered, and for some reason found myself lying. 'I don't. I don't have anything for him. He's okay, that's all. A bit full of himself, in fact, and...' *Don't mention vampires, Em.*

'You blush like a tomato when he pays you any sort of compliment,' said Jordi drily.

'Do I? Well... fine. He's okay to look at. But that's all. And tomatoes don't blush.'

Jordi smiled, although there was a sourness to it. 'We'll say no more.'

But there was more I needed to say. 'I only ever talk with him on the class Zoom calls and the WhatsApp group. I've never chatted to him one-to-one or anything. And I go red when *anyone* pays me a compliment.'

'Wouldn't be my business if you had chatted to him privately.' With that, Jordi folded his arms and seemed to draw a line under the topic.

Polly shifted in her chair, smirking weirdly. 'Well,' she said, as the silence cloyed and I tried to hide the fact I was rattled, 'my mum knows the head at Pebblestow Primary; Mrs Goddard – Helen – and she's really nice. Definitely not a megalomaniac. By the sound of it, she's nurturing an entirely different culture there than you've been used to.' Polly commanded Jordi's attention again. 'And it might be worth you having a chat with her. At the very least, she could offer some advice.'

Jordi took this in. 'Maybe.' His mouth relaxed enough to smile properly again. 'Thank you.' His gaze was warm, and I knew I ought to feel vindicated – he obviously liked Polly; as I'd known he would – but all I felt was cold and tired. And excluded again.

'As a last resort,' he said, glancing in my direction, a puckish look in his eye which I was suddenly irrationally grateful for, 'I could always get a job at Hartfield School. I'm sure they'd be happy to have me.'

'Oh, yeah,' I scoffed. 'As a male under thirty-five, they'd love you, Jordi. But then they'd proceed to eat you alive.'

'Tasty.' Polly laughed, and checked her phone. 'Right. I know it's not that late, but I'm shattered and I've got an early start tomorrow. I promised Sallie I'd help her with a sort-out at the café before we open up.'

'I hope you're being paid for that,' I said.

'Of course. Sallie wouldn't diddle me.' She looked towards Jordi. 'The meal was lovely. That steak was cooked to perfection; wasn't it, Em?'

I had to concede he'd done a good job.

'Still okay to drive?' Polly confirmed with him. 'I can get my mum to come, if—'

'No,' he cut her off. 'I'm more than happy to take you home, as long as you give me directions. I can find my way back with the sat-nav, if it's too complicated.'

'It's easy. And thank-you.' Her smile was radiant.

I wondered if they'd sneak in a little kiss, or a peck

on the cheek at the very minimum. Was it too soon? Polly could be devil-may-care at times, and excessively demonstrative; traits which up to now I'd admired in her.

Scraping back my chair, I grabbed my phone and tightened the denim jacket around me.

Jordi followed suit with the chair-scraping. 'We'll drop you off first up at the house, Em.'

'Oh,' I stammered, 'you – you don't have to; it's not far, and it's a nice evening.'

'It's no problem. I'd feel better knowing I'd got you home safely to your dad.'

'Well, that's very chivalrous, and possibly chauvinistic, but I walk around the estate on my own all the time.'

Polly squeezed my arm. 'Just say yes, Em. I'd feel better, too.'

For goodness' sake. I sighed with a dash of drama. 'All right.'

It was easier just to give in, although I didn't want to be in the back of Jordi's car, watching them ensconced up front like a potential couple, even for the minute or so it would take to drive up to the Hall.

Pathetic and perverse of me, but I hated feeling like a gooseberry. I was more convinced than ever that I was envious at never having had such a powerful mutual attraction myself.

It had never seemed to matter before. I'd simply accepted it. But now, on this balmy night, made for romance, I didn't want to have it rubbed in my face that other people would get to have all that and I probably never would.

The prospect of living vicariously had rather abruptly lost its bloom.

Chapter 19

Mulling things over was overrated.

I was determined, for my own peace of mind, to avoid it for now. But *not* mulling things over depended on distracting myself, which hadn't been easy the last few days, and had forced me to prowl the house and grounds finding things to do while I avoided straying anywhere near Donwell Cottage. If Polly and Jordi were meeting up, I wasn't going to pry. It was up to them to make their own arrangements now without my assistance.

On the day the gardeners were in, it was too beautiful a morning to waste indoors trying to evade my father, who was threatening to get out the shredder again, so I took myself off to the most secluded spot I could think of, where no one but me bothered to come.

The Walled Garden hadn't been tended to in decades. As a child, I'd used to pretend I was Mary Lennox and this was the eponymous secret garden. Weeds and shingle paths and mossy stones all around me, I'd daydreamed about things that seemed silly and inconsequential now.

Once, like many things around here, this space would have been very different. I'd found faded photographs and sketches and notes, and could have recreated it, if I'd wanted, in all its former glory. But... the effort it would take. And for what?

Dad and I didn't need to grow our own produce. The nearest farm shop had opened years ago and quickly cultivated a thriving business; deliveries were regular and economical, our loyal custom maintaining the routine my mother had begun.

While Mum loved flowers of all varieties, growing vegetables had never appealed. The Walled Garden had already been left to nature back then. Every so often, she used to remark they should do something about it, but Dad had just shrugged in that way of his, and neither of them had been motivated enough to stir the other to action; which had suited the old me, as I'd drifted with my daydreams around my own ivy-smothered wilderness.

Today, I propped my phone on the edge of a cracked urn that I'd dragged in here for this very purpose, and followed my dancercise routine with an unfaltering lack of co-ordination. But no one could see me, and I needed to burn off excess calories and confusion. When I was agitated these days, I tended to overeat. Exercise helped get me back on an even keel. Running wasn't my thing, but bouncing and flailing to music had always been fun. For about five minutes, when I was ten, I'd wanted to be a ballerina.

'Graceful,' said someone with unconcealed laughter.

I jumped, though not intentionally, and spun round, only to be met with a Leafley's uniform and a full-on smirk.

'Sorry,' he said. 'Didn't mean to scare you.' To his credit, he sounded as if he meant it.

'What are you doing here?' I demanded hotly, grabbing my phone to close the app as it loudly urged me to feel the music.

Zachary Martin held up his hands. 'No need to snarl. I'm paid to be here, remember?'

'But not *here.*' I indicated the Walled Garden. And it was a gross exaggeration to say I was snarling. Wasn't it?

He dug in his pocket and pulled out a pack of cigarettes. 'I just needed somewhere to hide. This doesn't fit with the Leafley's brand. I should be whisking out a flask of herbal tea or something.'

He'd invaded my private space for a quick ciggy break?! But I was unwittingly intrigued by the 'snarl' I detected in his own voice, and tempered my reaction.

'It's not as if you're a health guru,' I said, with a toss of my head. 'It's the plants that are supposed to be in peak condition.'

'True. But my... boss – the almighty – or Mr Leafley to you – doesn't like his employees looking less than hale and hearty.'

'He doesn't want you to blend in too much with the uniform, I suppose.' I stared pointedly at his green polo shirt.

'No.' He shoved the pack back in his pocket. 'That's fair enough.'

'You don't have to stop on my account. I can let you fill your lungs with toxic fumes at a safe distance.'

'It's okay. I'm trying to quit anyway, to be honest. Not successfully. I don't smoke much. It was a habit I should never have got into. But when you're a kid, and you want to stick it to your folks, or just fit in at some basic level with everyone in your peer group... right?'

I neither agreed nor disagreed. If he'd met my peers at Hartfield School, born with all those silver spoons in their mouths, he might have understood. 'Does Polly know?'

'About this?' He tapped his pocket and nodded. 'She stands back at a safe distance, too. Smart girl.'

'*Woman.* And I'd hate to see her hurt.'

'Is that a veiled threat? Hope you're including your mate in that, too. Though he seems a decent bloke. You fancy yourself as some matchmaker extraordinaire, as my mum would say. Don't you?'

To my surprise and dismay, Polly had evidently been blabbing to Zac.

But it wasn't a crime to want the best for someone. There was no need to defend myself.

'I know Jordi,' I said. 'I don't know you.'

'Right. Fair enough. You know Polly, though?'

'Of course,' I flared.

'She's not in the market for anything serious. She made that clear to me from the start.'

'And I bet she was even more appealing after that. An attractive woman who has no intention of sinking their claws into anyone. Every man's fantasy.'

He blinked at me for a while from under his cap, no deferential doffing today, either, then clearly decided he might as well say what he'd been thinking. 'For someone who claims to know a lot about romance and relationships, you don't have a scoobies, do you?'

I had no answer to this. He was only reiterating what I'd already accused myself of.

'Some men actually want to settle down,' he went on. 'But at the right time, with the right person. It can be simple enough – or the most complicated, messed-up thing ever.' Was that a clouding of his eyes I noted? 'I don't blame Polly for not wanting to rush into anything. So, we're not. It isn't like that. Do we fancy each other? Yes. Are we doing something about it? Not in any great hurry.'

'You've got no objections to her seeing Jordi, then?' I said, my curiosity mounting.

'Polly and I have never said we're exclusive. And I'm not sure I'm the one who'll be the most put-out, if they do hook up.'

'What do you mean?' He couldn't have read my mind. I was determined not to go there myself. All that jealousy stuff had to be shut away in some dark place where it couldn't intrude on the start of something wholesome and good. For Polly and Jordi's sake, I needed to be neutral and let it all work out as it ought to, with minimal interference from this point onwards.

'Nothing,' he replied at last. 'I ought to get back to work.' But Zac didn't turn away immediately. 'Can I ask one thing, though, totally on another subject?'

'I... suppose.'

'Why is this area so neglected?' He looked around us. 'I don't get it. Compared to everywhere else.'

I shrugged, debating whether to tell him. But the up-keep of the gardens was his business as a Leafley's employee, and I couldn't complain that he was asking.

'It was like this when I was small. Some of the Midwyn-ters were less financially astute than others,' I admitted. While I had a natural pride in most of my ancestors, there were two or three I only had contempt for. 'The Hall and grounds weren't always so well kept.'

'Shame this spot's still like this, though.'

'Well, seeing as I'm also the "below stairs" these days – which is how I like it – I get to have a say, and things might change. The cook would have made use of everything that was grown here once, and the produce from Home Farm, when it was still ours.'

'But nowadays there's Ocado?'

'The farm shop on the Bridgely road, actually. They deliver.'

He nodded. 'They've got good stuff. My mum likes it, too. But the orchard here,' he probed, 'that's still doing all right. What do you do with all the fruit?'

'Trees are more low-maintenance, and your crew han-dles the pruning. Besides, they're not tucked behind a high wall, out of sight, out of mind. The farm shop takes the surplus off our hands.'

'Fair enough.' It seemed his catchphrase. He stared around again, as if assessing the space. 'Have you heard of community gardens?'

'I've heard of them,' I said slowly.

'If you don't mind plebs on your land, it might be worth looking into.'

'I've never called anyone a pleb. Who do you take me for?'

'Mistress of the manor.' He met my eye, and there was a challenge there I didn't dislike. 'Queen of the castle.'

'Bourgeois bitch up her own arse?'

'You said it.' But Zac laughed, and I relented slightly.

'A community garden's an idea,' I said, with caution. 'One of many.'

'I can do some research for you, if you want. Look into it more. No strings.'

'Why would you do that?'

'Because, despite what you think, I'm not a complete bum, loser, deadbeat, or anything that might come under a similar heading.'

'I never...'

'I have to get back to work.' He tipped his cap this time, and I felt thoroughly chastened.

Zac Not-Efron might have more layers than I'd initially assumed.

Chapter 20

'As clouds scudded across the sky—'

'What colour was the sky?' interrupted Jordi gently.

'Umm...' Hetty floundered. 'Azure?'

'What colour is azure?'

I tried very hard not to yawn as this was going on, and took advantage of the fact we were on Zoom and I could pretend to be absorbed in my own notes.

'Blue,' said Hetty.

'But what sort of blue?' he coaxed. 'What kind of blue can people relate to?'

Your eyes, I thought, with a deep, buzzy, carnal feeling, and then almost sent my notebook flying as I jerked upright in my chair. Where had that come from?

'Cornflowers?' Hetty was suggesting. 'The blue of the Union Jack? That's too dark. Um... the sky? Oh, no, that's what I'm meant to be describing!' She laughed, all aflutter. 'So silly! You're all so good to put up with me.'

Meanwhile, I was all aflutter myself. No, no, *no*. This

had to end here. Right now. Non-platonic feelings *this* intense should never accompany any thoughts about Jordi's eyes. It didn't fit with our friendship. Okay, so we weren't siblings, Mum had been right, but it was still stomach-turning.

Or it ought to be.

But rather than any squirminess, there was only the acknowledgement that, yes, Jordi was good-looking. Futile to deny it. Therefore it wasn't all that absurd to be reacting to it now, as any woman might, even if I'd often preferred my men to have a dark and dangerous magnetism about them, like Frankie; although his capacity to make me blush had diminished recently. I wasn't keen on his sly jabs at Nancy-Jane. Her work wasn't to my taste either, however enviably well written, but I wasn't being mean about it.

Anyhow, back to Jordi. I stared at him studiously on the screen. In gallery view no one would notice, and besides, he was our tutor, it was perfectly natural to focus on him.

My breath caught in my chest, as a heady and intoxicating wave of lust – there was no other way to classify it – swept over me.

Damn. And a string of worse swear words.

This was inconvenient. *More* than inconvenient.

But was it a surprise, from an animalistic perspective?

The levelheaded part of my mind sprang into action, clutching at any reasonable excuse it could conjure, as I tried to calm the other parts of myself down.

It had been a long time since I'd been close enough to a man of my generation to unconsciously detect the pheromones wafting from his skin. Zac didn't count; I'd never gone for his type, personality or physique-wise, and maybe pheromones got diluted and dispersed easily in the open air.

Jordi shouldn't count, either, but he was *here*, and more accessible (in practical terms) than ever, and without my realising I must have been in his company indoors long enough to soak up whatever chemical enticements he was unwittingly giving off. It was basic science. They made documentaries about it.

I chewed my thumbnail, recalling that a vast number of animals undertook their procreative pursuits in the great outdoors, so my theory about dispersed pheromones seemed shaky.

Right, well, never mind. Much as it pained me, all I had to do was continue to avoid Jordi. Which I was already managing relatively well.

Not my intention when I'd first heard he was coming to stay, but things had changed on a number of counts. It wouldn't be fun to have him around if I was going to tie myself up in knots after every encounter. Sooner or later he was bound to notice, and how embarrassing would that be? He'd probably go out of his way to avoid *me,* then, and I needed to beat him to it.

Whenever he called in on Dad, I would just have to make some excuse and disappear. My compromising biological reaction might wear off soon enough, and then everything could go back to normal.

Except it couldn't, I remembered, because there was still that jealousy to contend with...

'You're miles away, Em.'

Snapping to attention, I blinked at all the faces on the screen.

'Are you all right?' Jordi went on.

I swallowed, my throat dry. Why was he picking on me? Had I looked that distant? Given myself away? 'I'm not... er... feeling very well,' I mumbled. 'Headache...' I tailed off, hating to lie in this context.

'Do you want to carry on?' Jordi frowned.

'With the session?'

'There's only a half hour left.'

'Oh.' I rubbed my left temple. 'Perhaps I should hunt down some paracetamol.'

'Get an early night,' interjected Frankie, somehow making it sound salacious rather than solicitous.

'Mmm. Catch you next week, then.' I apologised to everyone and logged off, sighing as I found myself alone with my rampaging thoughts.

I couldn't even message Polly and vent to her. She was part of the problem.

In a burst of despair, I stalked to the kitchen, and found things to wash up and put away, to keep me occupied. I reorganised a cupboard, while I was at it.

I couldn't think of any better plan than pretending I was under the weather to explain why I was distancing myself. All so pathetic. I was old enough to be able to deal with this rationally. But then, that had never been my strong point.

There was a short corridor from the kitchen which gave on to store-rooms, a pantry, and a boot-room. The door beyond, leading to the courtyard, was the one I tended to use on a daily basis rather than the formal front entrance with the heavy oak door and fancy portico. Tonight, I jolted at the sound of soft rapping, and peered down the corridor, where a shadow moved beyond the small pane of glass.

My heart slammed around my chest for a moment, but I padded to the door calling, 'Hello?'

'Em? It's me. I was just out walking and saw your light.'

Reluctantly, yet with an odd eagerness, too, I drew back

the bolt and unlocked the door.

'Hey,' I muttered listlessly, remembering I was meant to be unwell.

'Actually, I'm lying,' said Jordi. 'I wasn't just out walking. I came to check how you were. I was hoping I'd see signs of life, or I wouldn't have knocked.'

'Oh. Well, Dad's in his study, and that's on the other side of the house.' I pulled back the door. 'Do you want to come in, then?'

'If you're sure? Shouldn't you get some rest? Are you running a temp?' Without asking, he pressed the back of his hand to my forehead. 'You look hot, but you don't feel it.'

I stepped away. This was ridiculous. I'd attempted to hug him not all that long ago, and now I was doing my utmost not to get too close.

He followed me into the kitchen.

'Tea? Coffee? Cocoa?' I offered.

'I'm fine. Are you sure you're okay? Is it honestly just a headache? You've hardly been answering my messages. Or Polly's, either.'

'You've been conferring with Polly, have you?'

His brow furrowed. 'We've messaged. And I met her for a drink in Pebblestow last night. Her mum was there, too.'

Wow. Okay. 'Fast mover.'

'It wasn't like that. Blodwyn regularly pops into the Tarnished Key for a drink and a chat with the other locals.'

'Ooh, "Blodwyn" already, is it?' I forced myself to make light of it. 'How do you like your future mother-in-law?'

His brow stayed furrowed. 'She's a lovely lady. Like her daughter. But don't get carried away.'

'I like getting carried away. And I think it's wonderful.'

'If it's all so wonderful, why are you avoiding us?'

'I'm not avoiding anyone. I've just been busy – and headachy,' I put my own hand to my forehead, 'and I keep forgetting to reply. That's all.'

He stared at me for a few moments. 'What do you do if you need a doctor? Do they make home visits here?'

'I haven't needed anything that can't be discussed and prescribed over a phone. But old Dr Perry still comes out to see Dad, and his daughter's a GP locally, so we're sorted on that score really.'

'Good. I guess.'

'You guess?'

'You've got everything on tap. No need to push your-self—'

'To leave the estate?'

'Look, I know it's not that simple.'

'No. It isn't. And I'm not going to discuss it with you at this time of the evening, especially with my head the way it is.' I put a hand to my brow again. Ironically, it was going to start throbbing any minute, the stress it was under.

'Sorry.'

'I know you mean well, Jordi.'

He pulled a cranky face. 'Story of my life. "Jordi means well, *but...*"'

'But some things you can't fix, as much as you'd like to. And I'm not sure your ex-boss would have praised you that way.'

'No, fair point. And talking of work, I've set up a meeting with Helen Goddard. Just for a chat.'

'The head at Pebblestow Primary? She's bound to have some advice.' I recalled Polly telling him much the same, but with more warmth.

'That's what I'm hoping. A little guidance, maybe. A different perspective on things.'

'It's not as if you can expect anything more. Can you? You're only here on a temporary basis, so...'

'Well, I'd hardly stroll into another job *that* easily. But I'm not fooling myself I'll be able to stay around Lancaster, whatever happens.'

'But... your mum and dad?'

'The last few days, I've been speaking with Mum a lot. And Matt. It looks like my brother might be more fed up with the Big Smoke than I realised. And I haven't given Mum enough credit lately for being self-sufficient. She says I fuss too much, too. Besides, if I can help it, I'll never be further than two or three hours away.'

I found myself searching his face more intently than seemed fitting, trying to gauge how serious he was. 'Your flat – it's rented, isn't it?'

He nodded. 'If I decide I'm not going back, Matt's talking about maybe moving in. The landlord's great; we could come to some arrangement.'

'So you're sticking around *here*, then?' I felt some swell of emotion I couldn't identify. But I was panicked by the intensity of it, which might have leaked into my voice.

'Would you prefer it if I didn't?' His gaze snared mine.

'You can do what you want, Jordi. Whatever's right for you.'

'*If* I stay in the area, I obviously wouldn't expect to live in Donwell Cottage for free, but should you decide to rent it out...'

I could picture it now, Jordi and Polly and their life of domestic bliss at the end of my drive; albeit a much longer drive than the average person, so it wasn't as if I'd be stumbling over their idyll every five minutes. But had he really fallen that hard and that fast he was already contemplating resettling in Shropshire?

I hadn't even dared write such a strong attraction in my story. I'd been sensible and restrained, considering how much I'd wanted it to happen. I cared about them both too much, and it was one thing to bring two nice, decent people together, convinced they would work well as a couple, but another to rush them into a precipitous commitment. This wasn't fiction, and I wasn't out to wring as much emotion and drama from it all as I could get away with.

Jordi was still waiting for my response. And I was trying to come up with something apt to say, but it felt as if he'd thrown a live grenade into my head. My thoughts exploded off in all directions, and I couldn't form the words.

In the end, I didn't have to. My father came in, having heard voices on his way to the downstairs cloakroom, and expressing both surprise and delight when he realised who it was.

Jordi turned to Dad, though his smile seemed forced.

'Hi, Henry.' They'd caught up already the other day, and now Jordi had to explain what he was doing here this time of the evening.

'Emmeline isn't well?' My dad turned to me anxiously.

'What's wrong, darling? Do we need to call Dr Perry? I saw him at the club a couple of weeks ago, you know. Did I tell you? He's got a new putter. Anyway, you've been outside rather a lot, lately. Maybe you've caught a chill?'

'To be fair, Em,' said Jordi, 'your immune system probably isn't that great, these days. You don't get much exposure—'

'Look,' I cut them both off, 'I don't have a chill, Dad. I'm not sure people get those any more. And, Jordi, my immune system could be a lot worse. I have Polly bringing me bugs on a regular basis, and the cleaners, too. Even Dad wanders back from the clubhouse with the odd virus for me, now and again, though he won't own up to it. But the best cure for this might just be a good night's sleep.'

And to get away from them as soon as I could, to gather my scattered thoughts.

Jordi's lips contorted, as if holding back a laugh, which would have been ill-timed. 'I'd better be going.'

'Really?' sighed Dad. 'You won't have a nightcap with me? You're so like your father – has anyone told you that? There's so much of Dean in you, from the old days... We liked to sit with a whisky and put the world to rights.' He sighed again as my heart crumpled.

Jordi checked his watch. 'I'll stay for one, Henry.' His tone was gentle, and I cast him a grateful look.

He managed an open, amiable smile in return, before telling me he hoped I'd feel better soon.

I nodded wordlessly and escaped at last.

Chapter 21

Having Jordi's parting look stuck in my head was a problem, and I didn't know how to eradicate the image, or the heat that swept through me relentlessly as I lay in bed that night. Yes, it was a warm evening, and possibly I was at that point in my cycle when I was more susceptible to hot flushes, but however hard I tried to deny it, I knew there was more to it.

Perhaps if I concentrated my attention on his inner life... on everything he was going through, and how I could possibly help... it might divert me from how he looked and smelled and—

Remember the cheesy feet, Emmeline. And all those other dubious stenches I'd grown up with. Not his current scent, or the way it wafted around him alluringly...

I pushed aside the duvet, and lurched across to my desk. It was Polly's attraction to Jordi I needed to work on, not my own – fleeting (surely) and perhaps-not-so-ridiculous-when-you-took-everything-into-account – response.

If I'd ever fancied him in the past, I might have thought more of it, wondered if there was something in it, but I'd had plenty of chances to feel this way and he'd never stirred anything on this scale in me before. Ergo, it meant nothing in the present.

Nothing except the fact I must have been repressed for ages, and simply buried it among all my other problems. Those pesky pheromones and hormones were to blame now; nothing else. I could live with that. I'd get a grip on myself and definitely not on Jordi.

Damn. Why had I even entertained that thought?

I stuck out my bottom lip and blew air up into my fringe. *Enough.*

Staring at the blinking cursor on the laptop screen, my fingers hovered over the keyboard, waiting. A pose I'd struck many times before. As Emma de Wynter or Emmeline Midwynter? But they were one and the same. And I could face up to that, or continue to deny it, to my detriment. Either way, whoever and whatever I was, there was magic in my fingertips. I had the power to transform lives. An immense responsibility I couldn't, shouldn't take lightly.

Jealousy, desire, confusion – no, not confusion; I was now perfectly aware what was going on – had to be pushed aside. Like clouds in the sky, they weren't a permanent feature, however mesmerising or intricate. They would change, blow away, disappear.

It was the most prudent, balanced conclusion, and I poked out my chin, pleased with myself for reaching it, because all I'd had to do was admit Jordi was turning me on; end of.

And in light of that, and how superficial it really was – how meaningless in the grand scheme of things – I could get past everything else.

'A community garden might be a good idea, don't you think?' Polly leaned towards me over the bistro table in the back garden of Donwell Cottage.

Now that I was 'feeling better', she'd insisted I come over for drinks and nibbles. Jordi could have asked me himself, but seemingly he'd left it to her. A good sign, I told myself. He was allowing her to play host, and I'd arrived to find her lounging around the kitchen in shorts, boho blouse, and flip-flops, her hair flicking in various shades of honey around her shoulders. Happy and at home already. And Jordi also looked more relaxed than I'd seen him in ages.

All good. All fabulous. My pulse would slow down

soon enough in his proximity, and if it didn't, at least they couldn't see it.

Polly's mum would be picking her up, so we could all indulge in some Malbec. I wasn't sure it was a good idea to let my guard down, so I'd eaten a substantial dinner earlier and resolved to keep my alcohol consumption to a minimum and my mind reasonably clear. But I hadn't factored in quite how hard this would be. Despite the spiel I'd been consistently feeding myself for days, I felt excluded and depressed again in their company.

By the sound of it, she hadn't stayed over yet. Which brought me more consolation than it ought to. Nothing amiss, or inauspicious, in taking things slow, though. Their 'ship' was still really new – not really a 'ship' at all yet, in many ways – and if they wanted it to develop into something serious, there was a lot to be said for holding back and savouring the anticipation.

Polly had brought up the subject of the community garden. Zac must have mentioned his conversation with me. I clearly hadn't given it as much thought as he had. He'd gone off and done the research, as he'd said he might, and now it seemed Polly was trying to glean how significant a project it could turn into if I got on board with it. But I'd been distracted recently, although I couldn't publicly admit why, so opted to just shrug and say I didn't have strong feelings either way.

'It's got potential, if handled properly, but I don't think Dad would go for it.'

'Maybe if Zac spoke to him,' suggested Polly, 'his enthusiasm might rub off?'

'Don't you know my father by now, Poll?'

Jordi was taking all this in, pensively massaging his jaw, the stubble glistening like gold dust. I had to drag my gaze away, and dip into the gourmet crisps, as a diversion.

'Em,' he said earnestly, 'if anyone can bring him round to the idea, it'll be you. But you have to back it yourself first.'

'Obviously.'

I wondered why he wasn't more put-out with Polly spouting *Zac this* and *Zac that*. Mr Martin was evidently still a threat to their fledgling 'ship', but Jordi didn't appear fazed by it. There didn't seem to be even a hint of jealousy. Was his acting as good as mine?

While I tried to keep my expression neutral, it was draining what was left of my brainpower to sit here unpicking the ins and outs of a project that might bring about a lot more change than my dear parent would be comfortable with. He wasn't getting any younger, and his world beyond Midwynter Hall was shrinking year by year. Mirrored by me, to a certain extent. Although I'd once been more outgoing than my father in his youth, I seemed to be on a worse trajectory than him right now. I shouldn't bring any more stress into our lives if I could help it.

And yet... I couldn't say a small part of me wasn't intrigued, or up for a bigger challenge. I didn't *want* to be selfish any more when it came to the Walled Garden, and if I could use it for good, for giving something back, rather than simply me taking and taking all the time... I couldn't dismiss the idea outright. I just needed time and energy to think it through properly.

'Zac says there are loads of different reasons for starting one,' Polly enthused, 'beyond just planting veg and herbs and stuff. Of course, growing food isn't a bad thing. But you could have a sensory garden, too. Or a mini nature reserve—'

I grunted. 'It's already wild enough to be one of those.'

'Seriously,' said Jordi, 'the way I see it, the point of it's in its name.' He was encouraging me to look at him, lowering his head in an attempt to catch my eye. '*Community* garden.'

I took a gulp of wine, and met his gaze head-on. 'Strangers, in effect, tramping all over the estate. Can you honestly see Dad going for that?'

He made a sweeping motion with his hand, which I

suddenly visualised touching my face, stroking my hair, caressing my...

I shivered, focusing harder on what he was saying.

'Henry aside, Em, how would *you* feel about opening up the grounds more? The Walled Garden's on the east side, you could have a secondary drive or track branching off towards it. People don't need to go all the way up to the house. There are ways and means of ensuring you still get your privacy. And we're not talking crowds here. You're not advertising the place. You can set limited opening hours, issue access passes, whatever it takes to make you and your dad feel safe and in charge. But the main plus point about this, Em... if you can't go out into the world, maybe the world – or a small portion of it – can come to you?'

For a long moment, I didn't respond. But then: 'So it wouldn't be open to the general public?'

'According to Zac, it doesn't have to be,' said Polly. 'A shared garden could be purely for people from nearby villages who might get the most benefit from it. Not everyone in Pebblestow has a proper outdoor space; take my mum's cottage, for a start. You wouldn't be asking random horticulturalists from all over the place to just turn up and wander round, admiring the exotic shrubs and flowers or whatever else you decide to grow. It would be so much more than that. A hub for locals to come together and connect.'

'A hub? That sounds a bit too "new-fangled" for Dad. I'd have to phrase it differently.'

'A club, then,' said Jordi, adding wryly, 'he understands the concept of those, I'm assuming?'

I nodded slowly, munching on the crisps, as cogs turned more efficiently in my brain at last. 'If I related the whole idea to like-minded people enjoying a shared pastime in the open air, he *might* be able to grasp it...' I swung round to Polly pleadingly. 'But please, I need more time to consider it. Tell Zac not to get too carried away. I'm not good with pressure.'

She squeezed my hand. 'Sorry. I just think it's got so much potential, I'm getting carried away myself.'

'I know, it's okay.'

But the last thing I needed was to lose control of the situation. Who knew what it might trigger?

As Jordi cleared away the empty wine bottles, glasses and bowls a while later, and disappeared into the kitchen, I took the opportunity to lean close to Polly. 'It's going well, then? You and...?' I nodded towards the back door.

Her eyes clashed with mine before dancing away again. 'He's an incredible man. And I enjoy his company. So I'll grant you that much.'

I made an effort to look smug. 'See! And that'll do for now. If it's got legs, then there's no rush. Jordi's going through a major upheaval; it's not the ideal time. But if it's meant-to-be, in the long-term... You could be happy with him, Poll.' I swallowed a lump in my throat, and shifted in my chair. 'Thing is, though – by the sound of it, you're still seeing Zac.'

'Honestly,' she said gravely, 'I'm being straight with both of them. I wouldn't lead either of them on, or give anybody false hope. You know me better than that.'

'Of course.' I glanced towards the back door. 'I just... I don't want him hurt again. Jordi doesn't deserve it. But he falls hard, and too easily, I think, and—'

'Ironically, I'm not sure you know *him* that well, Em. When it comes to the women he's dated, how he's felt about them, I don't think he was really in love with any of them. He might have wanted to be, for his own sake as well as theirs, but...'

I blinked in surprise. 'He's said all this to you?'

'He's confided a little. I'm piecing together the rest.'

'Oh. But he's always been so... *sad* when things have ended.'

'Well, exactly. Wouldn't you be, if you wished something could work, but fundamentally...' she shrugged, 'it just never could?'

'I don't...' I was at a loss to understand.

Why couldn't Jordi make a relationship work? Why did he fail, the harder he seemed to try? He could be a dream man for so many women. What deep-seated issue did he have to prevent it? And had I put Polly in jeopardy, if she started to feel more for him than he could feel for her? But *why* couldn't he feel it?

I had so many *whys.*

I needed to know, though, to have some notion of how to correct it in my story, even if I did seem to have an abrupt case of writer's block, going by my latest attempts. Or at least, a case of wanting to go off on a sharp tangent.

What was wrong with Jordi's heart that made it so impenetrable in that respect? Because I knew how generous and open it was when it came to his family and friends; how easily he showed us how much he cared. Could it really be as simple as the fact he hadn't met the right woman yet? People fell in love with the wrong person all the time. It was one of life's universal lessons, and one of its most double-edged, too. Not that it had happened to me. But I'd been witness to it, so I must have some idea.

Don't go there again, Em. I rebuked myself, tired of treading over the same ground. And something struck me, as I sat in the sweetly scented garden under the string of warm white solar lights.

My inability to fall in and out of love might not be so rare after all.

There I'd been, speculating and judging, when all the time I was possibly just the same as Jordi. Because I had a biggish heart when it came to my family and friends, too. But no man I'd dated had ever won it; even temporarily. Or rather, I'd never been swayed or tempted enough to give it away.

Polly was consulting the Find My app on her phone, pulling me out of my thoughts. 'Mum's coming. She'll be here any minute. If you like, Em, she can drop you back up at the Hall?'

'It's fine.' Jordi spoke from the doorway, making me jump. The hairs at the nape of my neck tingled. 'I can escort Em back up, seeing as she likes walking so much.'

I was about to snap that I didn't need 'escorting' anywhere, thank you very much, when I stopped at the deadly serious look in his eyes, rather than the teasing one I was sure would be there.

I found myself nodding and gulping. 'Thank you.'

'Great.' Polly grinned, oblivious it seemed to the strangely charged atmosphere that had suddenly descended, and started gathering her things.

Chapter 22

We watched Polly drive away with her mum, the car turning into the darkness of the country lane and the tail lights disappearing from view.

Her goodbye with Jordi hadn't been any more effusive than with me. A warm hug for each of us and a hiccupy giggle. And then she was gone, and Jordi and I were alone, and in spite of the mild wine haze, I'd never felt more self-conscious or electrified in his presence.

I hated it.

I wanted what we'd always had. Silly and irreverent, annoying each other to distraction, encouraging and supportive, easy and unaffected, the happiest of times. I wanted to worry about him, and want the best for him, without all this other nonsense getting in the way.

'Is it really true you haven't set foot beyond these gates in two years?' Jordi asked, his voice quiet but somehow filling the silence like nothing ever could, or ever had before.

'*Over* two years. Although... that's not strictly true.' I ventured beyond the stone pillars. 'I can do this.' I took a step further, and then another, until I was standing in the middle of the lane.

Somewhere, an owl hooted. I swayed giddily as I turned to face Jordi, and in one swift movement on his part, I was somehow by the gates again. Still gripping my arm, he pulled me back further.

'I get it. Thanks for the demonstration. But standing in the middle of a road like that isn't advisable.'

'I don't see much traffic.'

'It's still a road, Em. Come on, let's get you home.'

'Fusspot.' I shook him off, and started walking up the driveway. 'I hate to see what you would have been like, if you'd ever been around for one of my panic attacks.'

'I wish I had. If only to understand them better.'

A beat of hesitation. I hadn't expected this answer. 'What's to understand?' I said truculently, gathering my wits together, or what was left of them after this evening. 'My head spins, I feel like I can't breathe, everything blurs or goes dark. Some people might think they were having a heart attack. I've never fainted or fallen to the floor, but everything's out to get me, and I can't deal with any of it. As if my fight or flight reflexes over-react and can't make up their mind what to do.'

'That doesn't make you weak, though.' Jordi sounded emphatic. 'You might have buckled or cracked, but that doesn't mean you're not strong, Em.'

I had no comeback to that. Could it be, for once, he wasn't expecting one?

Stumbling on the bumpy drive, I righted myself fast, but he took my hand regardless and tucked it into the crook of his elbow as if I was wobbling in a dangerous fashion. 'Maybe you had a drop too much Malbec.'

'Damn, you're judgey. I'm not drunk, Jordi. I'm nowhere *near* drunk.' Maybe if I was trollied, I could relax; though I'd probably make a fool of myself in other ways. Instead, tension made me stiffen, but I couldn't extract my hand. It felt at home there, as if it had finally found somewhere it wanted to be.

He sighed. 'Actually, Em, I was hoping for this chance to talk to you alone tonight. Because I owe you an apology.'

I stopped censuring and tormenting myself, and looked at him, instantly intrigued. 'What for?'

Jordi slowed his pace, until we were practically at a crawl. 'It goes back a few years.'

'Now I'm beyond curious. What did you do?' I couldn't imagine him committing any transgression against me.

For a few moments, it didn't seem as if he was going to say anything, but then he started up again. 'Matt and I have been talking, you see. I think this thing with Dad has thrown him for six. More than he was letting on until now. He's been having some long discussions with Mum, about life, love, the universe... You get the idea.'

'Heavy stuff.' My brow scrunched. What did this have to do with me?

'Anyway, a couple of nights ago, Matt admitted to me that he... well, he said he'd embellished some of the stuff that he'd got up to in London. Not recently, but back when he was an arse. His words, not mine. I don't think he realised the full impact of it all, till his conversations with Mum.'

I could feel Jordi's muscles tensing around my clammy hand, and something – a need to console and reassure – made me press my shoulder against his so-solid arm and say, 'It's okay. We've all behaved like arses at some point or another. We should give Matty a break.'

Breath left Jordi's mouth in a rough, frustrated hiss. 'I suppose. And that's why...'

'Why what? Why can't you just say it?'

'I thought he liked you,' Jordi gabbled, jarring me with his abruptness, and the plaintive note that hung in the air long after the words faded. 'And I thought you liked him,' he gabbled on, after a stunned pause. 'For a while, I thought you were... together. Not for long, but long enough. And I've let myself believe it all this time. Because it was safer, I guess.'

'What?' I spluttered, confusion like fluff in my brain. 'Me and... Matty?'

I managed to pull my hand away, and stopped walking altogether, swivelling to face Jordi. Moonlight filtered through the trees, complementing the lights set into stones at intermittent points along the driveway.

He shoved his hands in the pockets of his jeans, and kicked at a pebble; his gaze everywhere except on me.

'Are you joking?!' I wasn't sure why I should be so shrill or shrewish, except that the notion of Jordi believing I'd had a fling with Matty was making my stomach churn. 'Eww... What gave you that idea...?'

'Because Matt never denied it. Because I got it into my head that you were sleeping together.'

'Jeez! *Stop.*' I shuddered, my face puckering. 'That would never have happened in a million years. You and Matty are like brothers to me.'

The instant I said it, the moment that last sentence left my lips, I cursed and berated myself. I might have felt that way once, as a child, when people mistook us for a trio of flaxen-haired, brattish siblings, but somewhere along the line I must have moved Jordi out of that category and into another zone entirely. The friend zone, I had to admit, but that was infinitely better in light of the way I felt right now and the fact I wanted to slam him up against the nearest tree and kiss the living daylights out of him.

My face grew hot. 'I mean... I never saw Matty any other way. And I don't know what he led you to think, but...'

'It was when I came down to visit one time.' Jordi spoke quietly again, but with a hollowness that made me yearn to put my arms around him and tell him everything would be all right, that nothing could be as bad as he'd imagined.

It was a strange duality, to want to rush at him with a frenzied ardour yet smother him in a comforting, unconditional embrace, too.

'You were having a launch party,' he clarified.

'In that little book shop? The one near Covent Garden?' I nodded. 'I remember a few of us went on to a bar afterwards, but it was just you and me left at the end. That was the night you were off your face, and you almost started crying, and I had to take you in a taxi back to your hotel. If you'd deigned to stay on Matty's sofa bed... but you were too precious for that.'

'It was bloody uncomfortable. I could never get any

sleep.' His gaze flitted to mine. 'You'll never let me forget that night, though, will you?'

'In vino veritas.' I *almost* smiled. 'Or in beerum veritas, in your case. Anyway, the way you were rambling on, you were absolutely drowning your sorrows. You hadn't long broken up with that teaching assistant. Goodness knows what you'd got up to in the staff room. I'd always thought that was a bit incestuous...' I tailed off, biting my lip.

Polly's words from earlier crowded back into my head, about Jordi never having been in love. Recalling that night out in London now, though, the way he'd carried on, she had to be wrong.

'I wasn't upset over her,' Jordi muttered. 'We weren't even together that long, and I wasn't the only bloke she was seeing. I was off my face, as you put it, because Matt had managed to insinuate that he sometimes stayed over at your place, and I'd convinced myself it meant more to both of you than you were telling yourselves, even though you were trying to keep it secret—'

'Stop. Stop all of this right now.' I held up my hand. 'Matty crashed on my own very uncomfortable sofa *once*, as I recall, because he'd lost his keys after some party which happened to be round the corner from my flat. But that was *it*. I felt sorry for him, and ironically really wanted him to get his priorities straight, while deluding myself I had mine all figured out. But I have no idea how or why he ever thought I fancied him, except his ego has been massive for years. And I think you were right about what you said the other day – he *was* trying to bask in my glory.'

I took a breath, frowning at Jordi. 'But you should have asked me, rather than believe everything your brother told you.'

'I know.' His voice was small now. 'I'm sorry. That's why I'm apologising.'

'I can't hear you,' I lied.

'I'm apologising, because the very idea of you and my brother together, in that way, was...'

'Well, of course! It makes me want to vomit, too.'

Jordi snorted, but grew serious again almost instantly. 'Matt's sorry he never corrected me; that he let me go on believing it. He thought I'd forgotten, or that it didn't matter any more. He asked me to apologise to you on his behalf. But I told him he has to say it to your face one day, when he gets the chance. We've got enough cowards in the family. And I obviously don't mean my mum and dad.'

'So, you mean *you*?'

'I should have talked to you back then. I just went home to Lancashire and tried to forget about it. And that was a mistake. And me being gutless. Because I've never been able to forget. If I hadn't run... if I'd stayed on longer, and discussed it with you – then maybe... maybe I could have protected you more.'

I stared at him, at a loss for what to say. What did he mean? How could he have protected me?

'I feel partly to blame, Em, for what happened to you. For you being here, like this.' He gestured around us. 'Stuck.'

'Jordi.' I stepped towards him, sensing his distress again, and desperately needing to assuage it. 'This wasn't your fault.'

'But if I'd stayed and listened to your own version of it all, things might have been different. For both of us. Everything might have changed. That was the problem, though, you see. I was scared, I think. To take the risk. I couldn't shake off the worry that things would change for the worse, not the better. So maybe, what Matt said... maybe I warped it for its own ends. Because it was the best get-out clause my subconscious could come up with.'

I dared to touch his arm as a staggering thought stirred in my head. A burning question. 'Jordi, what could possibly have been different?'

His eyes met mine and held on, at last. 'When I'd come down for your launch, I'd been planning... I was going to ask you out on a date. You and me. A drink. Dinner. Whatever.'

A flood of intense heat. A breathless fluttering in my chest. Everything I'd been struggling against. It was all rushing at me, drowning out everything else. I couldn't resist it. But this wasn't a panic attack.

'A *date*, date?' I just about choked the words out.

'Yeah. One of those. You've heard of them, then? So what would you have said?' Crossing his arms defensively, he issued the challenge with a coldness that didn't suit him and seemed to come out of nowhere.

'If you'd asked me out, back then?' I owed him the truth. Evidently, we were both opening ourselves up to ridicule right here, right now, and I didn't want to be a coward, either. 'I would have said no, Jordi. Because I don't think I would have been ready to see you in another light. I would have been... shocked, and probably handled it really badly. So you were right to be scared. It might have changed everything. And not for the better.'

He sucked in his breath, but he couldn't hide his pain. The sting of rejection was like an old scar I'd never noticed before. 'Right.' He lowered his head. 'Thank you for being honest. For not sugar-coating it.'

'Wait, though.' I pulled at his sleeve, demanding he listen, because now that he'd said all that, now that he'd unlocked a door and we'd walked through it, it was impossible for me to step back out again. 'I've more no-sugar-coating to come. Or more honesty, rather. We're both older...' I moved so close I could feel the fever in him, his height and breadth. 'No wiser probably, but... the way I see you *now*, there's nothing holding me back from doing this...' I traced a finger across his cheek, gasping inwardly as the darkness flared in his eyes: a surge of longing, drawing the same from me, too. 'Or this.' I leaned into him, my mouth inches from his.

Jordi pushed me away, but didn't let go. His voice husky, raw. Fierce in the softest way. 'Em, you've been drinking.'

'So have you. We've still managed to have a rational conversation up till now. Or at least – it made sense by the end.' I stepped close again. 'It's okay,' I insisted, with an urgency I'd never felt before. Never *wanted* to feel, I realised, with anyone except him. 'I'm allowed to see things differently. It's fine for me to want this too... isn't it?'

His gaze searched my face, and must have found what it needed to see. When it dropped to my lips, I felt the tang of victory, the rush of anticipation.

And our first kiss happened as if by some great design in the grounds of Midwynter Hall. Clumsily at first, as

I pulled him closer and his arms tightened around me. But within seconds, it was so much more than anything I could have written. Mind-blowingly lovely. Thrilling and exquisite and oh so unmistakably right.

Pure passion was a fire, but it was the sweetest fire.

We came up for oxygen.

'Em,' he murmured, as if he'd waited a long time to speak it that way, to smooth back my hair as he said it.

'Jordi,' I whispered, losing myself in his eyes, in the possibilities I saw waiting there. Because I'd never said his name that way before, either.

Chapter 23

I padded around the kitchen in my thin summer dressing gown, daylight streaming relentlessly through the high windows. Emotions washed over me in waves. Joy. Disbelief. Fear. Guilt... The full gamut from light to dark. Perfect happiness and acute misery. And an addictive blaze from my head to my toes that was something else entirely.

Organising the breakfast things seemed mundane but necessary. A daily habit to focus on, diverting my attention outwards.

'Ah. Good-morning, darling.' My father clattered in and, without ado, took his customary spot at the table. 'We're being spoiled with the weather – just look at that sunshine.'

I squinted, blearily wishing I could dial it down as I settled opposite and offered him a toasted crumpet.

'I didn't hear you come in last night, Emmeline. Did you have a good time?'

He chose to ask this just as my phone pinged and vibrated on the table beside me. I gave a start, and flushed so intensely I was probably the deepest shade of red possible, short of being sunburnt. 'Er... yes, thank you.'

It was the first time I'd attempted to use my voice that morning. To my dismay, it was barely a croak.

My father looked up with a frown, as I'd feared he would. 'That sounds nasty, Emmeline. Are you coming down with something else already? You've only just got over the last one. How are your glands? Do they feel swollen? Maybe I really should get Dr Perry here to check you over—'

'Dad,' I cleared my throat, and managed to sound marginally better, 'it's fine. I'm fine. It was just... a late night, that's all. A bit too much wine and good company.'

'Ah.' He nodded, but continued to watch me as I forced myself to drink some tea. 'You look like you barely got any sleep. I hope Jordi doesn't make a habit of keeping you up like this.'

I almost spat the tea back into my cup.

'Not good for anyone's health, Emmeline. Staying up so late.'

'No.' I coughed. 'You're right, Dad.'

As he reached for the butter, I took advantage and discreetly flipped my phone over to check my messages.

—You escaped.

Accompanied by a row of sad face emojis.

I slid the phone into my lap, took a bite of my crumpet for appearances' sake, and tapped back:

> —I had to be here for breakfast. Dad would have worried even if I'd messaged him.

> —I know. You should have woken me up though. I'd have walked you back.

> —Because that was such a success yesterday?!!

I knew well enough what would have happened if I hadn't sneaked out, unnoticed, from under that monochrome tartan duvet at Donwell Cottage. It had been easier tearing myself away while Jordi was still asleep and unable to tempt me into staying longer. I'd just about made it back in time to shower and dash down to the kitchen, my hair damp, and my face shiny from the all-essential moisturiser.

—Sorry not sorry.

A pause. I didn't know how to reply to that. My phone pinged again.

—Em, are you sorry?

Of course I was. Just not for the reasons he thought.

—Never xx

It was safer to allay his fears. This wasn't the time to stir up paranoia in anyone, my father included, who was studying me from across the table.

'Are you chatting with Polly? Don't think I don't know what you're doing under there. You can hide your phone all you like.'

Bringing it back out, I rested it by my plate. 'Randall's coming with Mum today, isn't he? It seems ages since we saw them last. The longest gap we've had for a while.' Best to change the subject. I couldn't deal with thoughts of Polly, or how happy she'd looked yesterday.

I was guilty of a terrible betrayal. Far worse, in my mind, than anything Jordi had done. What I felt for him transcended any anger I could have directed his way. It was somehow all reserved for me. I was an awful person. Selfishly trashing a precious friendship. But Polly couldn't have reproached me any more than I was reproaching myself.

'Oh, I asked Jordi over for lunch, too,' said Dad. 'I sent him a text a couple of days ago.' He looked proud of himself.

'What?' The croak was back.

'Well, it seemed ridiculous to have him so close and not ask him. He's practically family. Surprised he didn't bring it up.'

I waited till Dad was faffing with the teapot, pouring a second cup, before sneaking my phone under the table again.

—Are you coming here for lunch today?
Dad says he asked you.

—Is that OK? I forgot to mention it.

—Of course...

I could hardly tell him it wasn't. His paranoia would have gone into overdrive.

...but can we not say anything to them yet. About us. I need time to let it sink in without everyone sticking their oars in. The whole thing just blew me away. I'm still dazed I think.

—Was I that good?

He added a winky face emoji.
I played along.

—You want me to score you out of 10?

—Let's just call it an 8. It gives me something to aspire to.

I blew out a breath, my face aflame, to match the rest

of me.

'I really think it might be an idea to call Dr Perry,' my dad remarked, frowning, 'I don't think I've ever seen you this flushed, Emmeline.'

I took a swig of tea, giving myself a few seconds to come up with an excuse. 'I don't need a doctor, Dad. It's only ladies' issues.' Which hopefully might silence him on the matter. 'My hormones are in flux.' It wasn't exactly a lie.

Dad pursed his lips and shook his head, as if he highly disapproved of hormones and everything that came with them. 'Well, your mother will be here in a few hours; you can talk it over with her. I'll keep the men entertained, don't worry. Maybe take them to the driving range,' he added, with a twinkle of excitement. 'Jordi did say his swing needed working on.'

It took a few more messages with Jordi, while I got dressed and ready, until I was satisfied he wouldn't intentionally give anything away. When the time came, however, and we were all assembled in the dining room with its sunflower yellow walls and sumptuous brocade drapes, the old walnut table polished and the cutlery gleaming, even I was finding it difficult not to let something slip accidentally in either a look, word, or gesture. For one thing, in spite of my remorse, I still wanted to throw myself into his arms and flee with him to the cottage; to the perfect space where it was just the two of us, impermeable and in the moment.

'This is very...' Jordi stared around the high-ceilinged room, but seemed to flounder for the right words. As he met my eye across the table, I knew his lack of speech had nothing to do with the warm vintage grandeur.

'We only ever dine in here on Sundays,' said Dad. 'I'm not one for dinner parties. But Emmeline had it decorated so beautifully, it's a waste not to use it.'

'All we need is a footman or two, rather than getting up and down ourselves,' I tried to joke. 'See? I forgot the gravy!' I pushed back the heavy chair across the Persian rug.

'Do you need a hand?' Jordi straightened in his own chair.

I cast him a glance that hopefully said *tone it down* but would be untranslatable to everyone else. Which I dare say was asking a lot.

My mother and Randall had arrived at the Hall before him, Jordi turning up a short while later. He had kissed my mum's cheek and shaken the men's hands, but then stepped on my toes as he'd tried to simultaneously kiss me and pump my hand, in a moment of blundering indecision.

Thanks to his lack of coordination – which definitely hadn't been a problem last night – my toes were still throbbing and sore. And now my dear mother had her eyes peeled on both of us, so that any interaction, even passing the horseradish sauce, felt loaded.

I tried to steer the conversation towards her and Randall, and their plans for the summer, but she was too wily and kept looping back to Jordi, taking a particular interest in his upcoming meeting with Mrs Goddard, headteacher at the junior school in Pebblestow.

He was keen to learn more about a possible transition from secondary to primary, but he had no expectations beyond that. 'I'm finding it... liberating,' he said. 'Taking each day as it comes. Working on various options. Polly put me in touch with the husband of a friend of hers; he has a background in teaching, too. I've already met him for a drink.' Jordi stabbed at a roast potato. 'A lot of food for thought, really.'

'It certainly sounds that way.' My mother smiled. 'I'm pleased you're moving on, in a professional sense. You were treated appallingly and you deserve a clean slate. You look... happy now, Jordi. I'm so relieved to see you like this. And if you ever need any business advice, from an entrepreneurial point of view, Randall would be more than glad to talk to you.'

My stepfather concurred with alacrity.

'And speaking of moving on...' Mum was smiling again, 'how are things going with Polly? Emmeline said she was going to introduce you. My daughter's convinced herself she's nothing less than a modern-day Aphrodite. Goddess of love.'

Jordi's eyebrows were saying far too much for comfort.

'Meddling in the lives of us mere mortals,' added my mother. 'Though sometimes getting awkwardly mixed up in it herself.'

'To be fair,' said Dad, conspicuously unaware of any subtext, 'a young, single chap like Jordi here could do a lot worse than Polly Evans. Lovely girl.' He turned to me, bristling with concern. 'Are you all right, darling? That cough's come back! Jordi, son, could you pour her more water, please? Thank you, thank you. Now drink up, Emmeline. If this carries on, I'll definitely be calling Perry to come check you over. No arguments.'

Randall, seated next to me, was patting my back. I couldn't even bring myself to look at Jordi now, who was opposite, next to my mother.

'I'm sure it's nothing serious, Henry,' said Mum. 'Allergies, at the very worst. I don't think you need to bother

Dr Perry.'

I nodded, and guzzled the water. 'Allergies. Definitely.'

Chapter 24

·♥·♥·♥·♥·♥·

Jordi followed me into the kitchen. 'We need to tell them.' He was helping clear the table, as Mum held court over coffee with my father and Randall. 'I don't understand why we can't. It feels wrong to let them think I'm seeing Polly.'

'Aren't you?' I put down a pile of dishes by the large butler sink.

Jordi followed suit with his own dirty crockery, then turned me to face him, squeezing my hands. 'Em, *no*. Where's this coming from?'

'From the fact I kept announcing I was setting up my two best friends, and until yesterday, they'd seemed to be getting on really well. Everyone thinks I'm right, for once.'

'So you'd prefer to keep what's happening between us a secret, so that everyone carries on thinking you're the world's best matchmaker?' He let my hands slip from his. 'Which is bollocks, by the way. You're arguably the worst.

If you couldn't even see how I felt...'

It hadn't escaped me that all those 'tells' I thought I'd been so shrewd at noticing might have been deliberate or exaggerated, because it wasn't a stretch to think he'd been letting me win at cards, or whatever else we'd been playing.

All that time when I'd thought one thing, while something else entirely had been going on...

Was it any wonder I was dizzy and defensive?

'I'm not *that* proud, Jordi. It's got nothing to do with me getting everything so catastrophically wrong. I don't care on that score. It might even be funny, in a really dark way, if it wasn't for you feeling like crap all these years thinking you might have been able to help more, and me bringing Polly into it right before I realise I want you for myself.' I pressed a hand to my head, and groaned. 'Shit.'

Moving back a few paces, Jordi propped himself against the hefty, scrubbed oak kitchen table. 'Polly and I are just friends. We made that clear early on; when I drove her home, in fact, that first night. She told me what she did and didn't want, and how you won't accept it when she tells you she's not ready for a serious boyfriend.'

'But, you were attracted to each other – weren't you?' Had I interpreted it so badly?

'I was just being friendly, for your sake, and then Polly

and I agreed we might as well get to know each other, so we could all hang out together comfortably. But you seemed to be avoiding us, after that, so I guess we both needed some company. It was *never* going to be in a romantic sense. Because, Em... whatever I'd been telling you, or even myself before I arrived here... the instant I saw you asleep on that sofa, it all went straight out of my head. I knew then, the more time I spent with you...'

My 'but' was a lot weaker this time.

'Everything you said about Polly, though... you weren't wrong,' Jordi acknowledged. 'She's a special person. And she deserves someone in her life who isn't hung up on someone else.'

As Jordi stared at the floor, I stood in silence for a long moment, gripped by pity and shame, frozen with regret.

He looked up, facing me squarely. 'That's one of *my* flaws. A pretty big one. Trying to ignore or forget how I felt by seeing other people. Not calculated or premeditated, as such, it was more complicated than that. I really, really wanted them to have a chance, and I put as much effort as I could into it each time. Gave them everything I thought they needed.'

'You picked terribly, Jordi.' I was compelled to say it. 'Rosamunde in particular. But all of them were wrong for you. Whether that was your subconscious again, trying to sabotage things, or whatever. But it's why I really wanted you to meet Polly. The grumpy-sunshine trope...' my voice tailed away.

'It's more obvious to me than ever, Em – there's only one woman who could ever be right.' He stretched out, pulling me towards him. 'And in spite of how much she drives me round the bend, it seems I've always preferred grumpy-grumpy. But we're not *really* that sullen or in-different – are we?'

His hands slid around my back. Despite myself, I leaned into him; his feather-soft lips burying themselves in my neck, kissing me softly, slowly, until I shivered, my bones turning to water.

'Stop,' I muttered, wriggling free. 'Not here.'

He laughed with a throatiness that kicked my pulse into a gallop. 'Where, then?'

'Not now, either. I wasn't suggesting that. You're so crude.'

Footsteps and loud coughing in the corridor made me spring back even further, though I was possibly beet-root-faced when my mother walked in, while Jordi strug-gled to suppress a less than innocent grin.

'Oh, hello, you two.' She smiled serenely, putting the tray with the coffee things down on the table. 'Busy clearing up the mess, are you?'

I swivelled back to the sink so she couldn't see my face.

'Jordi,' Mum went on, 'Henry and Randall are waiting for you. They seem eager to head off to the range. Emmeline and I will finish up in here. Thank you for your help, though.'

'Always my pleasure, Anne.'

He turned to me, and for an instant seemed to be about to kiss me, but stopped himself, and ended up rubbing my back, which might not have been any better.

'See you later,' I choked.

Even after he'd gone, I still refused to look round.

Mum came up beside me, and began scraping any remaining food off the plates as I filled the sink with warm suds to wash up anything that couldn't go in the dishwasher.

'I'm glad you both took my advice and stopped antagonising each other so much,' she remarked casually a short while later, picking up a tea-towel to start drying. 'You're treating each other like grown-ups at last.'

'There was never anything wrong with the way we treated each other, Mum.' I had to argue the point. 'If we hadn't both enjoyed it, we would have stopped years ago.'

'You think? Maybe Jordi didn't know how else to act around you. He never saw you as a sister, you know.

Regardless of how you viewed him.'

I was beginning to understand the implications of that. Forced to look over the past in a different light. There was something bittersweet about it, tinged with a sense of loss. Because while it was intensely flattering to think he'd been attracted to me for years, it also oversimplified everything positive he'd ever said and done.

All our past interactions seemed somehow more basic and less nuanced. Every motive, every action, every wish to 'help', was now tainted with the fact he was male and ultimately wanted to get me exactly where he'd had me last night.

Drying my hands, I shrugged stiffly. 'Well, it's nice to be good friends. Perhaps that's better than siblings. Less rivalry. Besides—'

'Sweetheart,' Mum cut me off, 'you can drop the act. I know you too well.'

'What act?'

She cupped her hand to my chin, lifting my face till I was looking her in the eye. 'You and Jordi.'

'What about us?'

'You know how he feels about you?' Her tone was soft, persuasive.

I had to give an inch here before she took a mile. What was the point in continuing to deny it? We'd been rumbled.

'I know he likes me,' I muttered. 'He's liked me for a while.'

Something mournful flickered in her eyes. 'Emmeline,' she said solemnly, 'Jordi McAndrew Daley *loves* you. He's been in love with you for years. It was plain to Deanna and me, even before it was probably clear to him. Calling it anything less would be doing him a disservice.'

I was about to refute this when a huge sigh shuddered through me, halting me in my tracks.

'Love?' I shook my head, though it lacked impetus. 'He hasn't said *that*... not exactly.'

'If he cared less, maybe he'd be able to talk about it more. Perhaps you both could. Because I suspect you've loved him for ages, too.'

'Me?' I shook my head again, but with vigour. 'I only started feeling this way over the last week or so.' Even as I spoke, I heard how silly it sounded. How pathetic. My moods had been tied up with Jordi's for far longer. And I knew we hadn't gone back to Donwell Cottage last night just to satisfy a passing need.

'Love doesn't always arrive with a big fanfare, Emmeline. Slow and steady can be just as wonderful, if not more so, because when you finally wake up to it... Oh, sweetheart, don't cry.' Instantly, she gathered me into her arms, and insisted on holding me as I let it all out. The tears, snot and despair. Pent up for too long. 'What's wrong?' she murmured into my hair. 'Aren't you happy? Why are you trying to hide it from the rest of us?'

'Because.' I sniffed. 'So many things! *Polly*, for one. She likes Jordi. And I kept saying how great they could be together. I truly believed it. She's exactly what he needs, except he'd prefer to be stuck with someone like me.'

'Emmeline, *no*. Don't say that. You mustn't even think it. You're an amazing person. And I'm sure Jordi's aware how lucky he is you feel the same way about him. Do you know how precious that is?'

'But the timing of it all—'

'If you wait for a "perfect" moment, it'll never happen. There's no such thing.'

I mopped up my tears with a clean tea-towel, and leaned back against the sink. 'He's going through so much at the moment, though.' My heart ached for him more than ever. But to some degree, his pain had always been mine. I couldn't recall a time when it hadn't.

'And yet,' said my mother, 'I've never seen him look so happy.'

'Mum! That's terrible.'

'Is it? In spite of everything he's going through, the woman he adores has just reciprocated his feelings. How do you expect him to feel, Emmeline? You're a writer; use your imagination. That's not to say he isn't still worrying about his parents or his career. Of course he is. But with you beside him, he probably feels stronger. Braver.'

'But I won't be – will I? Beside him. Not properly.' I gestured around me. 'This is my universe. It may have escaped your notice, but I can't be with him in his.'

A wrinkle formed on my mother's brow. 'He's here right now. That's what you need to focus on. With time... and with Jordi's help...'

'You think he can actually cure me?' I stiffened, hot tears behind my eyes again.

What was wrong with me? Had making myself vulnerable last night, naked in every possible way, opened me up to a new wave of hurt and anxiety? My body was very definitely screaming, *no*. My brain, however, fretted otherwise.

'That's why you're glad about this,' I said, 'because you think having him here will be some kind of quick fix. I won't try therapy like you want me to, so perhaps a relationship is the next best thing? I'm not sure the experts would agree with you. Bagging a boyfriend doesn't miraculously make everything better.'

'I'm "glad", Emmeline, *only* because it's obvious to me how much you both mean to each other. It doesn't seem you've had much chance to discuss all this between you, though.'

I stalled, remembering how Jordi and I hadn't done much talking once we'd got back to Donwell Cottage.

My temperature started to rise, my scalp to tingle, my skin to yearn for his touch. So typically inconvenient. And so typical of me. The best night of my life, and the day after, I was standing around whining, and selfishly wanting more of the same with no regard for anything else.

'You should try to talk properly,' Mum advised. 'I know it's easier said than done when there are other... distractions,' she punctuated her words with a delicate pause, 'but you need to make time to sit down together and discuss your relationship without anything else getting in the way, even the strength of your feelings.'

She ran a gentle hand over my hair. 'It's bound to be a bit strange at first after all this time, and if you want, I won't say anything to your father yet, or Randall. I doubt either of them noticed anything. Your father especially. He's content to be oblivious. If he had his way, he'd keep you here with him forever.' Her voice acquired a spikiness I'd heard before.

'Mum. Do you think...' I swallowed and tried again, 'do you think Dad doesn't really want me to get over the agoraphobia?'

Putting it out there, so plainly, I knew she would give me an honest answer.

She threw back her head for a moment, as if considering it, but I suspected she already had firm views on the subject, even if she'd never shared them with me.

'I believe he isn't doing it on purpose, Emmeline. Not in any scheming way, at least. Your dad exists in a bubble, too, and he's indulged you too much. Only because he's scared, I think, at the prospect of finding himself alone again. Not solely the notion of missing your company, but the fact you do so much around the place.'

'I couldn't leave him, Mum, and I can't see myself living anywhere else again but here.'

As my thoughts crystallised, I knew, with absolute conviction, that this had been true from the moment I'd returned. And even though no one had ever threatened to force me out of the Hall, my fear of what the outside world represented, my throat-constricting panic at finding myself alone and helpless out there, had meant that for the last few years, I'd had an incontestable excuse to stay.

'Midwynter Hall is your home. I don't think anyone who knows you and loves you, is going to ask you to leave. Not permanently. But, sweetheart,' Mum hesitated, 'you need to learn to straddle both worlds. You have to put your trust in professionals who understand your condition and how severe it's become, and can help you through it. Medication, CBT, whatever it takes. Because you deserve a full life. That's all I've ever wanted for you.' She tucked my hair behind my ears, pulling me into another hug as tears spilled down my cheeks again. 'And I'm more than certain it's what Jordi's always wanted for you, too.'

Chapter 25

A bird had started its lonely trilling even before the first glimmer of dawn brought colour back to the landscape. I stared unseeingly out of my bedroom window, high above my dark realm, a princess alone in her tower, chinoiserie wallpaper and ornate plasterwork all around, heart full of woe.

If my stomach hadn't been so knotted up, I might have chastised myself for romanticising the situation; for attaching glamour and drama to something so painful and perplexing.

The day hadn't ended on a good note. After Mum and Randall had left and Dad had disappeared to his study for an overdue nap, I'd led Jordi upstairs, and... well... I'd fully intended to take my mother's advice, and sit him down to talk on my favourite window-seat with its inspiring view, but faced with my four-poster, we'd given in to more primal urges.

It turned out Jordi had come to the Hall prepared, be-

cause apparently I'd stocked the bathroom cabinet at the
cottage rather optimistically, and he was taking the hint.
This could only have been my intention on a subliminal
level, I reminded him, tugging off his shirt, because I
hadn't been thinking of myself at the time.

And then, of course, once it was over, my mind turned
to Polly and what an awful human being I was. And I
began to cry again, prompting Jordi to beg to know what
was wrong as he held me tight in his irresistibly buff arms,
and I smeared tears over his equally toned chest.

But when I tried, I found I couldn't explain. The right
words wouldn't come. The fact he was exonerated from
any wrongdoing over Polly, having established between
themselves they were just going to be friends, didn't make
it any better on my part.

It actually made it worse, because I hadn't known this
last night. I hadn't stopped to consider Polly's perspective,
but tumbled headlong into Jordi's bed, propelled by my
own feelings. My own superior sense of having known
him first and longest, and thereby having the larger stake.

As if you could carve up a person that way.

I had no claim over him. His feelings were all that
mattered. His choice.

But he didn't understand what he was really taking on,
and I said as much, in slightly different words, as I tried

to squirm out of his embrace.

'You don't know what you're signing up for.'

Jordi pulled me back towards him, professing with a fervour that left me weak and breathless: 'It's a million times better than anything I've had before.'

And he kissed me again, held me, murmuring that I was his lighthouse. Because when he'd been out there on his own, lost at times, or thrown around in a tempest at sea, he'd kept me in sight, my light, to remind him where land was, where a safe harbour lay. Even if all it could ever be was friendship.

He was so exposed, talking like this, and all I could think was: some lighthouses warned of danger. They weren't just there to guide you home. Some blared out: *Stay away. For your own safety, don't come any closer.*

I must have been intent on subversion as I finally managed to peel myself away, pulling on his shirt just to have his scent near my skin. I fetched my laptop as he sat up and leaned against my pile of pillows, a dent in his brow.

'Read this,' I said. 'You asked me not to write it, not to "interfere", but I couldn't help myself. I'm stubborn and contrary. You need to know that.'

'You think I don't know by now?' But he gave in, doubtless out of curiosity, before I could say more.

I curled up on the window-seat and let him read in

silence, the groove in his forehead deepening, before he finally put the laptop aside.

'That's as far as you got?'

'Far enough, don't you think?' I padded back over to perch on the bed.

'Em,' he sighed, floundering momentarily, 'do you honestly believe all this stuff you wrote was coming true? There are a few similarities, some coincidences, but aside from that...'

'It wasn't just this story. There were others. They all came true, too. I tried to tell you, Jordi.'

'Jeez,' he hissed under his breath. 'You really were serious about that – weren't you?'

'You just wouldn't listen. I know it sounds... unbelievable—'

'It isn't so much that, Em. Though it's concerning, I can't say it isn't. But what I'm struggling to wrap my head around is that you actually think it's okay to do this. To manipulate people's lives this way.'

I flinched slightly. 'But – you don't think it's real, so why should it matter? According to you, I'm not doing anything except making clever assumptions and predictions and weaving them into a story. That's what you're saying it amounts to.'

'I didn't say "clever",' he pointed out drily. 'I wish you

could hear yourself. You're asking me to believe that all these people – me included – don't have any say in how we behave, or who we fall for, because you're sitting here in this room controlling us. We're basically at the mercy of your naive whims.'

'I wouldn't say *naive...*'

'Like something out of *A Midsummer Night's Dream*, you're going around sprinkling your love potions on us, albeit digitally,' he jabbed a finger at the laptop, 'and we're just your playthings.'

'But I stopped writing your story,' I protested. 'You read that far, didn't you? I couldn't bring myself to write any more, because I was getting too involved, wanting you for myself. So—'

'So what you're saying is, you *made* Polly like me, and then realised you were jealous and decided you had first dibs on me.'

'Yes,' I said meekly, 'but I didn't write myself into it that way.'

'You still can't see my point, though, can you?' His eyes bored into mine, before he finally scrambled out of bed and began pulling on his clothes. 'I'm going to need my shirt, please.' He kept his gaze averted as I took it off and slipped my dress back on.

'Jordi...'

'I'll make sure your dad doesn't spot me on the way out. I'm not in the mood to stay late, however much whisky he wants to ply me with.'

I sniffed, and rubbed my nose. But my eyes were adamantly dry now, as if I'd exhausted my daily quota of tears, though it felt as if I'd shed more than a year's worth.

Jordi turned back at the door, clearly vacillating, softening, in spite of himself. 'I'm not mad at you. I'm just...'

By now I was gripping one of the bedposts, attempting to look composed and attractive and every bit the Em he'd wanted all these years, more fool him. I probably looked a hot mess.

It was how I felt.

Before I could respond, he crossed the room in a few strides and enveloped me in a fierce hug, burying his face in my hair, swearing at himself. 'I'm not the sort of person who walks out on someone just after I've slept with them. And it's even worse when it's you.'

I squeezed him back, drinking him in. 'It's fine, Jordi. We can disagree, and you can be angry with me. I'm not going to hold it against you or call you an "f"-ing scumbag. Because I'm obviously the sort of person who can't just be grateful for the post-coital afterglow, and has to pick a fight or run away. Which is also worse because it's with you.'

He nodded, and pressed his forehead to mine. 'Talk tomorrow sometime, okay?'

And then he was gone, and the worst of my thoughts crowded in on me, filling the gap he'd left behind.

As I sat on my window-seat later, after tossing and turning for hours in a bed that could never feel the same again, I accepted that he wasn't pleased with me, whatever he'd claimed at the end.

But wasn't that what I'd intended, when I'd given him my laptop? Something theatrical and contentious, to ease my guilt at being so unfairly happy. Make him see what he was getting into. I hadn't expected his logic to overtake mine, but the more I thought about it, the more sleepless I became; the more agitated, because he was right.

However good my intentions, if I honestly thought my gift was genuine – whether or not anyone else believed it – my schemes were self-aggrandising and capricious, condescending and vain.

And *dangerous*.

Because if I'd typed myself into the story the way I'd found myself wanting to (however hard I'd tried to convince myself I didn't)... And if I'd written Jordi diverting his attention from Polly, to me, because deep down he'd carried a torch for years...

Then I never would have accepted the truth.

I never could have believed, for certain, that his feelings for me were real.

Chapter 26

Tiny particles of dust resembled constellations of stars against the blackness of my phone screen, as I sat waiting in the shade for Polly; too twitchy to even scroll through Instagram to see what Isabella's dog had been up to and which boujee collar the pooch was wearing today.

I couldn't stop wondering when Jordi would answer the text I'd sent earlier, although it hadn't said much except that I was sorry.

To be fair, perhaps I'd needed to be more specific. I could have been sorry about a number of things.

Give him space, woman. He clearly expected time and distance to get over this hump. And maybe he was giving me the same in return, to process everything that had happened over the last forty-eight hours.

Jordi was well aware he'd taken me by surprise with all this, though not in a bad way, and certain elements of my reaction had to be warranted. Also, if he knew me as well as he said he did – and I no longer doubted the legitimacy of his claim – he couldn't think it odd I was struggling to accept I could be happy.

In my present predicament, having messed up more things in my life than I'd realised, it was judicious to ruminate on my mistakes, and how, if at all possible, I could put them right.

Starting with Polly.

Which was why I was sitting on a bench in the Walled Garden, where she'd asked to meet.

Presumably, she wanted to discuss the community garden idea; and if it hadn't been for Dad, I would have granted her anything right now, even agreeing to the concept on the spot. I was so desperate not to fall out with her, particularly as I'd already come close to it over Zac.

My initial impressions of him had been snobbish and inexcusable. I'd been no better than the girls I'd gone to school with, even though I'd always thought myself their superior, with a refined social conscience.

You absolute dick, Em.

I'd been no better and no worse.

Actually, no. I *had* been worse, because I'd been so obstinately blind to my real flaws.

Many of the deficiencies I'd tended to pick out in myself were just fundamental human traits, and I hadn't seen my true self at all. Even now, I was probably missing half my faults.

'Em!'

I looked up as Polly bounced towards me, but she wasn't alone.

My stomach sank. I'd been planning to confess all to her; explain how I'd fallen at a pretty basic hurdle in our friendship. But I wasn't willing to bare my heart to her when she had Zac in tow, in spite of my growing regard for him.

Smoothing my features into a smile, I breathed back all the words I'd planned to say, bottling them up again.

I might not have been fast enough to hide my dismay, though. Noting the kink in Zac's own smile, and the way he shook his head, almost imperceptibly, it seemed he'd misconstrued my reaction. His cockiness from the last few times we'd met wasn't immediately obvious today.

'Zac's not at work, said Polly, 'so he gave me a lift. Sorry not to warn you.'

'Right.' I tried to broaden my smile; make him feel included. 'Hi, Zac. How are you?'

'Yeah. I'm okay.' He shuffled his feet, in what I couldn't help observing were a notoriously exclusive brand of trainers.

'We've got something to tell you.' Polly announced,

grabbing his hand.

Surely not. My jaw dropped. I blinked at them.

Polly seemed to realise what she'd implied, and instantly let go, almost pushing him away from her. 'Oh, heck, no! I didn't mean that.' She let out a belly laugh, shooting a look at the young man, who was reddening by the second. 'I was only holding his hand out of moral support. You see, Zac came clean last night, and I told him it was important for you to hear it, too. You shouldn't make any decision about the Walled Garden without knowing the full story. Should she, Zac?' Polly nudged him.

'Now I'm intrigued.' I injected calmness into my voice, attempting to mimic my mother.

'No,' he said, responding to Polly's prompt, 'she shouldn't.' He turned to me. 'I haven't been completely honest.'

Join the club. But I regarded him with an open, expectant expression, belying the maelstrom underneath.

'Bob Leafley,' he went on sheepishly, 'well... he's not just my employer. He's my dad.'

Polly's gaze ricocheted between me and Zac as if he'd just announced his father was Darth Vader. But after the shock of assuming they'd got engaged, anything else seemed tame. I lifted my eyebrows, nevertheless. It felt a fitting response.

'Big surprise, no?' gushed Polly. 'Zachary Martin – "heir apparent" to the entire Leafley's empire.'

The young man flicked his eyes skywards. 'And *that's* why I don't tell anyone when I first meet them; and why my mum and sisters keep quiet about it, too. It's not exactly an "empire", though, Poll.'

'It's close enough. But, anyway, do you want me to fill Em in – or will you?'

He turned his palm upward, and indicated for her to go ahead. 'You're enjoying this too much. I'd hate to spoil that for you.'

I bit back a smile, as Polly's sheepish countenance matched his own.

'Okay,' she said, but falteringly. 'Well. It seems people treat him differently when they find out.'

'I can empathise with you there,' I said, with feeling, and shuffled along the bench to make room for them. 'This isn't me treating you differently, by the way. But it sounds as if this could go on a while, and you might as well both get comfortable.'

They squashed next to me.

Polly was growing uncharacteristically bashful by the second, fiddling with her hair as she backtracked: 'I think it might actually be best coming from you, Zac.'

He didn't look at either of us as he nodded. 'Fair

enough.'

'Listen,' I said, 'don't feel obliged to say anything. You really don't have to explain yourself to me.'

He rubbed the back of his neck. 'I'd like to, though, seeing as I've been dragged along today to state my case or plead my cause or whatever.'

Polly sighed. 'I was just trying to help. You shouldn't feel embarrassed, if that's what's bothering you. Em's parents aren't together, either. And at least you know where your dad *is*. I have no idea what mine's up to right now, and I don't really care.'

I suspected she did, even if she couldn't see that for herself.

'Yeah, yeah.' Zac gave in. 'Fine.' He stretched out his long legs towards the wilderness of the Walled Garden. 'My folks split up before I turned one,' he began, 'though they were never married. And Dad was... *distant* after that, for a few years, building up Leafley's. Never totally absent, but maybe not around enough, either.'

Zac stared at the far wall, pausing for a moment. 'He never got hitched or had any other kids – too married to the business. So, he started trying harder with me as I hit my teens. Jealous of my ex-stepdad Ade, I think. But I wasn't that close to Ade, either; he had two daughters with my mum, and they sucked up most of his time and affection. I was a bit of a maverick compared to my sisters, and not in the best way. Anyway, I probably did a load of stuff I shouldn't have, before Dad got through to me, and we started to connect properly. I resisted going to work for him for ages, though.'

'And you still want to make it on your own, to a certain extent, don't you?' said Polly. 'That's why you're starting at the bottom, working your way up.'

He threw her an indulgent look. 'Correct. Plus I wanted to get my degree in horticulture first.'

'You have a degree in horticulture?' I sounded taken aback, and quickly checked myself. 'That's great. You should have said, though. Not left it till today.'

'I don't like to brag.' His smirk was entirely valid. 'And I won't appreciate how Leafley's is run, not properly, until I see it from every employee's angle. A BSc can't help with that.'

I admired his diligence. How could I have got this man so wrong?

'You want this project for yourself.' I gestured to the garden. 'To prove something to your dad?'

He didn't immediately reply, and I wondered if I'd misjudged him again.

'Yes. And no,' he said, eventually. 'I'd like the challenge and the responsibility, but I don't feel like I've got anything to prove any more. I'm already seeing things from a broader perspective and learning to share my opinion. Leafley's isn't a bad place to work, but it could be a *great* place with some adjustments here and there. I'm slowly helping Dad understand that. Implementing a few minor changes; nothing revolutionary. He's been set in his ways a while now, and I don't want to terrify him.'

'Like mine,' I sighed. 'That's the problem. The more I think about the community garden, the more I think it's a good idea. But I don't know how to sell it to my dad without him having a heart attack.'

'You're exaggerating,' said Polly, 'and Jordi would agree with me. Your dad could be persuaded without jeopardising his health.'

At the mention of Jordi, my stomach clenched, and I dropped my gaze.

'Your dad basically needs extra time to adjust, that's all,' Polly went on. 'And you know you could probably bring him round to the idea. Jordi was right when he said there are loads of ways to ensure neither of you lose any privacy up at the house, and you don't have to be involved that much, if you don't want.'

I already knew I wanted to play a part in it, though. How that might work was still unclear, but reinforcing my sense of purpose around Midwynter Hall couldn't be a bad thing, could it?

'Talking of Jordi,' said Polly, 'have you heard from him yet? Do you know how it went today?'

I regarded her blankly, even as my face filled with an uncomfortable prickly heat. 'What?'

'His meeting with Helen Goddard, at Pebblestow Primary...?'

Oh, damn.

'Em!' said Polly. 'You hadn't forgotten?!'

I was an even worse person than I'd been twenty minutes ago.

'Yes. I mean, no... No, I haven't,' I stammered, 'heard from him yet.'

Polly's gaze scoured my face. I hated to think how much remorse had to be etched across it, clashing with the redness.

'Well, he's probably still busy,' she said. 'It wasn't his only meeting today, after all.' She bit her lip as Zac prodded her.

'He had another meeting?' I said sharply. 'Who with?'

'Not a meeting as such,' Polly turned away from me, 'just another chat. It was nothing. Anyway,' she swept on, 'Zac, you haven't told Em the other reason why it might not be that much of a long shot, getting her dad to buy into the community garden.'

'Polly,' I said, still playing catch-up, 'who was Jordi—'

She jumped up, her relief palpable as a couple of figures came into view, ambling through the arch in the far wall.

I recognised my father instantly, of course, but with a lurch of consternation to see him outside the house, gesturing animatedly around the scrubby garden. He was rarely outdoors without his golf bag and trolley; but no, he didn't have his figurative crutches right now. Yet he looked lively and excited, and not at all anxious, even though he must have walked in the opposite direction from the golf club to get here. Which only heightened my own anxiety. This wasn't like him.

The other man was slightly younger and stockier, with a shock of greying blond hair. I'd met him before, when I'd first summoned Leafley's Landscaping & Garden Maintenance to the Hall to discuss a plan for the upkeep of the grounds. I couldn't help comparing him now to the tall and lean Mr Martin, who had to take after his mother in build.

'Zac,' I said, 'why is your dad here?'

'Emmeline, look!' my own parent called, before Zac could reply. 'It's Jigger Bob!'

I wondered if I looked as dazed as I felt. 'Sorry, what?'

The two men came to a stop in front of the bench, my dad still gesticulating excitedly. 'I've told you all about it, Emmeline. How Bob got the name last year – after winning the Jigger comp on the last hole. We partner up sometimes.'

I shrugged bemusedly, before my thoughts congealed into something unpleasant as another of my failings struck me. The fact that I never really listened to my father if he wasn't talking about anything of interest to me.

When he came in from golf, I must have perfected the art of looking as if I was paying attention. He would rattle off names, and spout on about competitions and scoring systems and handicaps, and a load of other stuff he must have assumed I understood, as my mind drifted off.

While I wallowed in my shame now, however, I realised neither Polly nor Zac looked surprised to see Bob Leafley here.

As if reading my thoughts, Polly enlightened me: 'We left Bob up at the house, Em. Your dad answered the door. He was really happy to see him.'

'But...' I shrugged, still at a loss to grasp what was going on. I merely sat there, while 'Jigger' Bob introduced Zac to my father.

There was a lot of manly hand-pumping, suddenly, and a strong whiff of old-boy-networking. Yet somehow, buried deep in all of this, I sensed the mysterious and magical hand of my mother.

If I had any gift or powers, it was quite conceivable they came from her. Midwynter Hall might merely be an innocent bystander.

Dad turned to me again. 'Have you heard about this commune idea thingy, darling?'

I was hit by a swell of exhaustion, as lack of sleep finally caught up with me, and I lost all grip on the situation. 'Community garden, Dad,' I said, lacklustrely. 'A commune's something else completely.'

'Yes, yes,' he nodded, 'Bob's been explaining it to me. It's his son's scheme. Fascinating idea. I said to him you'd take some persuading, though...'

I was about to speak when I felt my mouth clamp shut. My tongue caught up with my thoughts, and I sagged on the bench.

What was the point?

The point of being certain about *anything* any more – when all that I thought I knew, was bit by bit being turned on its head?

Chapter 27

·❤·❤·❤·❤·❤·

I stared at the phone as I sat at my desk.

—Sorry for not getting back to you sooner. I wrote a reply this morning but never hit send. I've deleted it now. I need to get my head around everything, and think maybe you do too. It's been a long day and I didn't sleep much last night. Can we talk tomorrow instead? Hope you're ok. You're always in my thoughts. x

Oh, yes, Jordi, I sulked, *I'm wonderful!*

But was that an attempt at a conciliatory note at the end there? An affectionate way to sign off, although it didn't fit with the general negative tone? Or was it a warning that he couldn't get my pride and misdemeanours out of his mind?

Between Jordi and my mother, they would have me believe I'd been a fixture in his thoughts for a long time. Half a lifetime, maybe. Which seemed so quixotic it barely made sense.

Of course, it was more than likely he'd woken up to the truth. Having finally 'caught' me, he'd discovered the hype didn't live up to the reality.

But was it possible to go back to the way things had been before, if that was the preferable option for him? Everything we used to have, but without the yearning-and-lusting-for-me part? Could I be enough again simply as a friend, and how would 'platonic' even work now that he knew what I really was?

Anyway. I could go round in circles for hours, but it was all by the by. It was *my* turn to see him differently. To want him so much it hurt. So *I* was the one who could never go back.

The bloody man had made me realise how much I loved him. Convinced me – as I lay snug, and frankly astonished, in his arms – that I'd found *the Spark* I never thought I'd feel. The classic soulmate connection.

By contrast, his own devotion belonged to the Em he'd carried around in his head all these years. That key fact was unassailable. Immutable.

I just wasn't sure that Em was me.

HOW AMAZING!!!

I frowned at the WhatsApp message that had just popped up. It seemed Hetty was about to be all aflutter about something, but I didn't have the patience or energy to get sucked in. Leave that to the others.

My laptop screen was blank, although I was meant to be working on the latest mini-assignment. As if I could focus on that! The whole course thing felt too weird now. How was I supposed to sit there and act normal for the entire Zoom call, knowing I'd seen our virile tutor naked, and not just because I'd accidentally walked in on him in a wet room once?

I turned off my notifications and flipped the phone over.

My nails were in danger of being chewed along with my pens, so I left my desk and mooched around the house, ending up in the conservatory, where I watched a misty drizzle blur the deepening twilight beyond the glass.

I hadn't had a chance to speak to Polly one-to-one today as I'd planned. All I could wish for, when I eventually managed to share everything, was that she was so loved-up over Zac all of a sudden, she didn't care I'd moved in on Jordi behind her back.

I could visualise Polly with Zac now without grinding my teeth in annoyance. I'd judged rashly and harshly, but intended to reassure him, going forward, that he had my respect and my apologies.

I was frustrated, however, that I hadn't had the opportunity to grill Polly on what Jordi had been up to in addition to his chat with Mrs Goddard. I felt sure I could have caught her out, made her slip up and drop some hint.

It was galling that she still knew things I didn't. Presumably she was privy to this information because Jordi popped in and out of Pebblestow without a second thought, compared to the debilitating anxiety that accompanied my own visions of doing the same. Anyway, as likely as not, he chatted to her while he was there.

I might have minded less, if Polly hadn't been so furtive about it. As if I wasn't supposed to know. If I asked Jordi outright, he'd realise Polly had blabbed, which wouldn't have been fair to her.

The lack of control, the sense that I was being bounced about like a ball inside a pinball machine – it had all soured today's success with the community garden project, which had brought us one step nearer – a giant leap, in fact – to convincing my father that I was fine with it, if he was.

Maybe, subconsciously, I was glad I hadn't talked with Polly the way I'd wanted to. It felt oddly like a reprieve. A stay of execution.

Urgh, Em. You're so dramatic. You should be a writer.

I'd heard those words as a child, never knowing back then that writing had value as a form of therapy. As I'd grown up, it had simply been an ambition, a goal to strive for. And I'd felt so clever and brilliant for all of five minutes that I hadn't seen the cold hard truth. Very little about the profession was equitable; none of it was easy; and you had to grow a far thicker skin than mine. In the outside world, you were only as clever as everyone else thought you were.

For a long while, more recently, writing had just reminded me of what I'd once had and how spectacularly I'd lost it. The only time I hadn't felt that way, was when I was working on my matchmaking stories. I'd had direction then. And although I understood why I needed to give them up, and the perils of believing in them, I felt empty now at having lost those, too.

No, not *empty*, because I was unquestionably miserable.

Which wasn't the best mood to be stuck in, when I returned to my desk, reached for my phone, and finally found out why the writing class was so excited.

Chapter 28

So. Frankie and Nancy-Jane were an item, were they? And they'd confided the news officially to Hetty first, so she could announce it to the group.

A whole thread of messages unravelled before me, explanations and congratulations, but I had yet to comment. Everyone might misconstrue my silence. Damn.

I had to get my thumbs into gear and fib a little.

> Oh, how fabulous! That's great news. Sorry I didn't reply sooner, my phone was on charge and I missed the notifications. So happy for you both. Such a surprise, but a really lovely one.

There was a lump in my throat.

It had nothing to do directly with the admission that Nancy-Jane had gone to stay with Frankie, after they'd been corresponding privately since the early days of the course. Or that they were planning to find a place together where they didn't have to rely on lifts to get about with their mobility aids. Or that they'd decided to keep a lid on it all until they knew how serious it was, and how they were a bit sorry about that, because sometimes Frankie had got carried away and acted like he didn't care.

As I picked my way internally through my reaction to the news, I soon reached the conclusion that I wasn't miffed in the way everyone maybe thought I was. In spite of Frankie having flirted with me, more than once, I was genuinely happy and hopeful for them, because finding someone you connected with to that extent was something to be cherished. I was only put out that I hadn't picked up on it. Then again, that was hardly a stretch if you considered I didn't have 'a scoobies' about relationships, as Zac had so eloquently phrased it.

But over the last few days, I'd been on a crash course, culminating in my willful throwing of a spanner into the works. And if only I'd done things differently, it might have made me the most ecstatic of women to announce to the group I'd found my own happy ever after, too.

That would have been stealing Frankie and Nancy-Jane's thunder, though, as well as being unprofessional with regards to Jordi.

And it was becoming apparent I hadn't found my

happy ever after anything. I had no elated announcements of my own. I could only fuss over Frankie and NJ, as he'd started calling her, and wish them all the best.

It was impossible to control what individuals in the group thought of me, or if they collectively suspected I felt chagrined by the whole thing. But I couldn't go on fearing what others believed; it would only ever be a half-life, however pretty and gilded it might seem. The only thoughts I could regulate were my own, and even that was hard enough much of the time.

As I put the phone back on the desk, I had a suspicion that admitting all this to myself was a first step.

One of many.

I had a long, and perhaps lonely road ahead. But the sooner I resigned myself to this, the sooner I could start moving forward.

The lump in my throat suddenly felt an awful lot bigger.

My phone pinged and vibrated as it lit up the bedside table. I grumbled as I groped for it, but it wasn't as if I'd been asleep, or even close.

—Em, are you awake?

—Yes.

—Are you ok?

I frowned, and lay back against the pillows, holding the phone aloft as I stared at the three words, wondering what they really meant.

—In what way?

I had to ask. Jordi could have been referencing several things. Or maybe that was the intention. He wanted several answers. In spite of his knackeredness after his 'long day', he evidently couldn't sleep, either.

—I heard about Frankie and Nancy-Jane. Hetty spilled the beans earlier. I think they meant for her to tell me. Apparently the whole group knows? Hope you're fine with it?

And what was that supposed to mean?!

—I wished them all the best. I don't care about Frankie that way, if that's what you're getting at. I hope they're very happy together. And just think, now you can promote your course as a dating service too! You're having more success than me.

—Glad they haven't hurt your feelings.

Was that all he could say? I was a wreck because of him, because of *us*, and he was worried my feelings had been hurt because two people I'd never actually met in the flesh had been hit by Cupid's arrows, and I'd been (only very slightly) caught in the crossfire.

I was about to type a passive aggressive answer, when the three dots appeared again.

—Look I know we need to sit down and thrash this out. I'm not baling on that, please believe me. But I've just arranged with Mum to go to Lancaster tomorrow

for a few days. Dad's had another seizure
tonight and I said to Mum I'd speak to
the docs with her and Matt. I'll take my
laptop and do this week's session from
up there. All being well, I'll be back by
the weekend.

Oh.

This was how it began. Or rather, how it ended. He
would have to go home to Lancashire more and more, if
he even came back from this trip.

All this need to escape to Midwynter Hall for his mental
health, et cetera, and he'd ended up in even more turmoil
– because of *me*.

And I couldn't help him. Couldn't go with him to see
Deanna, give her a giant hug and try to be there for the
whole family, the way I ought to be.

– Sorry about your dad. Please give your
mum my love. Tell her I'm thinking of
her.

Silence for a while.

– Of course.

Jordi, I love you.

I stared at the phone for ages before typing:

— Take care then. Drive safely.

Another pause.

— Always.

Chapter 29

Things were going from bad to worse.

I hadn't actually thought they could get worse, I felt despondent enough, but I clearly hadn't learned all my lessons yet.

I'd stoically logged on for the writing course as usual, though my eyes might have looked puffy and pink, however much caffeine serum and concealer I'd dabbed underneath them.

My contact with Jordi since he'd arrived back in Lancashire had been brief. He'd texted to say he'd got there with just a minor hold-up. And then, once he'd gone with his mother and Matty to the care home, he let me know they were adjusting his dad's medication, and he still planned to come back to Shropshire at the weekend.

I didn't know what he was coming back for, except his things were in Donwell Cottage, so he'd have to pick them up at some point.

Prolonging the agony wouldn't do either of us any

good. His family was up there, his roots, his real home, and I didn't doubt he'd find a new job eventually. His former boss probably had a reputation for being an arsehole, and there had to be more sympathetic headteachers and better schools within a twenty-mile radius of his flat.

We could chalk up our brief... whatever it was... to experience.

If we ended it quickly, before it got even messier...

I'd stop crying eventually. And Jordi would stop moping, find a sweet, authentic girlfriend, and make a relationship work long-term because he'd finally stopped obsessing over a woman who could never have lived up to his dreams.

There. All settled.

I was going to be a grown-up about it. I was virtually thirty; I needed to act like it.

His face appeared, along with all the others, in gallery view on my screen. And just the sight of him, the unmistakable trepidation as he faced us all, the shadows under his own eyes – I wanted to reach into my laptop and hug my friend for all I was worth. Because that was what I'd truly lost. My oldest, dearest friend. My own lighthouse guiding me to port.

'Emmeline,' said Cole, 'are you okay?'

I could see myself, a trembling hand over my mouth

as if I was about to throw up. Would everyone think I was heartbroken over Frankie? There he was in all his vampirish glory, sitting right next to NJ in person, both of them glowing with adoration, though looking more uncomfortable by the second.

'She hasn't been feeling well,' said Jordi quickly. 'Migraines. Em... it's okay if you want to give this session a miss. I just need to discuss one thing with you all before—'

Hetty cut him off, gabbling worriedly, 'Oh, Emmeline, no! Are you suffering again? I thought it was only a bug. But my mother used to get horrendous migraines when she was your age, apparently. Luckily I never took after her. You do look ashen. Maybe even a bit green. Jordi's right, you should give tonight a miss. Go lie down and rest...'

Jordi was frowning even as she waffled on, but he didn't interrupt.

Hetty finally wore herself out, and sat back in her chair.

I nodded and muttered, 'I'll go rest in a minute. I think Jordi has something he wants to tell us all first.'

I braced myself. This might not be good. His brows were twisted in apprehension.

'Okay. Right,' he began, rubbing his nose. 'Over the last couple of weeks, I've had two or three interesting

conversations with a small indie publishing house. It's
literally so new you won't have heard of it yet. And before
you get too excited, it's just a one-man operation, but he
has real vision. I think it's got potential to go the distance.'

My brain began to stir (beyond thoughts of how much
I wanted to turn back time when it came to Jordi and
me) as it latched on to his words and joined the dots.
Could he be talking about Polly's friend, or the friend's
husband and his new business, to be specific? Was Jordi
referring to someone in Pebblestow? That meeting he'd
had? When Polly had first told me about this new local
publishing venture a few months back, she'd assumed it
would pique my interest. Instead, I'd only realised how
strong my aversion to publishers still had to be, however
noble this particular indie press might sound.

It wasn't unreasonable to suppose I might always be
triggered by the memory of crushingly tight deadlines and
the strain of promoting my 'brand'; compounded with
the even greater pressure of sustaining it all, the more
well-known I got. I wasn't ready to jump back on the
hamster wheel yet – if ever.

'For a while now,' Jordi continued, clearly selecting his
words with care, 'I've been mulling over the idea for a
collection of stories with a common theme. I thought of
self-publishing, at first, which is still a viable option, but

this publisher's interested, you see—'

'Goodness!' Hetty couldn't help herself. 'That's wonderful! How much good news can we have in a week, I wonder? I didn't realise you wanted to write professionally, Jordi?'

'Me? No! No, Hetty. Like a lot of people, I've always been better at teaching than doing. I was talking about you. *All* of you. Featuring your stories in a group anthology.'

On my screen, everyone in the grid made 'O' shapes with their mouths. The regulars from the WhatsApp group; and the others I only knew as a face and a name, who were more reserved in general, barely even piping up during our lessons.

All dazed by what Jordi was trying to impart.

All except me.

I was too sceptical not to cut through the gloss, scrabbling for the tarnish underneath. 'Did you show him samples of our work, then? Or does this publisher think they can sell it, regardless of the quality?'

Jordi swallowed visibly. 'Em?'

That simple response spoke volumes.

'Are they relying on one name in particular to promote it,' I said; 'i.e. mine?'

It was a point-blank question, and he looked a touch

paler. 'Your name?'

'Emma de Wynter. *That* name.'

'Oh, right. Well, no. You can use another pen-name. Or just Emmeline Midwynter. No one has to masquerade as anything they're not.'

I pressed my lips together, and stared off to the side.

One by one, the others started to make noises again, animate themselves, ask questions of their own.

Apparently, Jordi had had the idea of calling it *Boxed In*. He wanted to amplify voices that didn't always get much of a say. Unadorned, honest stories, about physical and mental conditions which sometimes kept people detached from society, for a myriad reasons. Fiction blended with real-life experience. He hoped the narrative diary exercise he'd set us would have helped us all see how our stories had truth and validity. Even if we hadn't shared these in group discussions, he'd intended it to be a starting point, a fresh perspective on our lives.

The more he talked, the stronger his voice became, the more excited everyone grew.

'I don't remember giving you permission to show my work to anyone outside of this group,' I said, eyeballing the screen again.

'Sorry?'

'I think you heard me, and understood.'

My written words hadn't been meant for anyone else. I didn't want an outsider scrutinising anything I'd produced for this group, or work I'd sent directly to Jordi.

'The diary exercise was, and *is*, private,' he said firmly, 'and even though some of you asked me to cast an eye over what you've done so far, I would never have shared that. The examples I used were the best of your stories and poems and plays. Short sections, just to showcase your work. That's all.'

'You should have told us what you were planning when you first had the idea.' I was no longer the passive student, and if the others had all been in the same room together, no doubt they would have been looking among themselves with raised eyebrows.

There was subtext in my tone and attitude. Hetty, in particular, didn't seem to like it; wincing as if she were a little girl and it was her parents who were arguing.

'I'm sure Jordi just didn't want to get our hopes up,' she offered. 'It's so very difficult to get a publisher to notice you these days. More than ever, I think. And we could so easily have been disappointed. Even now, I'm certain we'll have to produce exemplary work if we want to be included in this anthology. I'm sure I won't know what to write. Or what I want to say, thematically. No doubt you'll all have to help me brainstorm—'

'Whatever you write, Hetty,' I interjected, 'it has to be shorter than *War and Peace*. And if the stories are in alphabetical order, Bates will be up first, so you mustn't send people to sleep before they've even had the chance to read anyone else.'

Hetty was slightly open-mouthed for a few seconds, but then her lips pinched into a rosebud and her gaze dropped to her desk. No one filled the silence. At last, she looked up again.

'You're right, Emmeline. I'm sorry. I do go on a bit, don't I? You're all very nice to put up with me, considering you're all streets ahead. I'm not sure my work will ever be at a publishable standard. And I'm only a carer; I don't have a condition of my own, as such. Not much to say. Maybe you'd better not rely on me, Jordi. The others will write impactful, memorable stories for you. You won't need mine.'

Jordi squared his shoulders, and looked broader and somehow more distanced from me than I could remember. 'Hetty, *everyone* will be included. I'm not leaving any of you out if you want to be involved. And I'll personally help anyone who feels they might be struggling. Besides, carers are some of the most forgotten people out there. It's vital you get a say.'

'Oh.' Her eyes looked watery. 'That's so very kind...'

She tailed off for once after just a few words.

'Em.' Jordi frowned. 'You had a headache, didn't you? You were going to sit this session out?'

I stared at my screen, simmering, and light-headed as if there wasn't enough air. He was such a hypocrite, accusing me of controlling people, of manipulating lives, when he'd done all this planning for the anthology behind my back. Behind all our backs.

'Yes,' I said. Practically a hiss. 'Sorry everyone. But I'll see you next week.'

And I left the meeting.

Later that night, I sat on my bed, stewing. I'd drunk a gallon of camomile tea to try to calm myself down, but now I just kept needing to pee.

He had no right. No right at all to share anything I'd written without my permission. Perhaps I shouldn't have let my anger get the better of me so publicly. And I had to concede I could have been more tactful with Hetty. But Jordi had got me more wound up than ever. He was so infuriating, and always so *worthy*. Such a knight in shining armour to every underdog that crossed his path.

And now he was FaceTiming me. Shit. I glared at the

phone beside me on the duvet.

Ignore it, Em. Don't engage.

I scooped up the phone and jabbed at the green button.

'What?' I snapped.

He grimaced back at me in silence.

'Jordi, you called *me*. What do you want?'

'What's up with you, Em?' The grimace wasn't going anywhere. 'Is this because of the other day? The stuff I said?'

'About me being controlling? Well, what do you think? But you're just as bad. You don't get to decide whether I publish any of my work. You shouldn't have gone off and done that.'

'This isn't just about you. And you don't have to take part if you don't want to. No one does. When you all signed up to the course, there was a clause in the terms that said I could share any of your work at my discretion, but everyone retains the copyright to their material at all times. Nothing will ever be published without a contract. Hetty was right, I didn't want to get everyone excited if it was all going to amount to nothing.'

I contorted my face, hating his self-righteous answer, an inconvenient stinging behind my eyes.

'And I understand now why you might have needed to write those stories of yours,' he went on, ignoring my stubborn silence, 'because you have no control over your phobia, so at least writing about people in that way keeps you linked to them, and attached to a world you can't face yourself.'

'Have you been talking to a psychiatrist or something?' I couldn't stand how patronising he sounded.

'No,' he retorted. 'My mum.'

I took a deep breath. Deanna might have a point. But I wasn't going to let Jordi revel in the satisfaction of having relayed it to me. I needed to wipe the smugness from his eyes.

'Wouldn't it have made more sense to talk to the one person who has a greater stake in it than you?'

For a second, there was a smidgen of what might have been contrition, before the grimace was back. At least that meant he didn't look so smug.

'And we will,' he said, with the most ominous of sighs. 'I promise, Em. And in the meantime, you should apologise to Hetty.'

'But she knows she witters on too much.'

His brow darkened. 'She didn't deserve what you said, though. Out of all of them, she's the one who likes you best, and probably feels the most awestruck. The sun shines out of your backside, as far as she's concerned. Hetty's a big fan of your books and of *you*. And you insulted her.'

'Jordi...'

'You're pissed off with me and you took it out on her, the last person you should have picked on. But I can't believe it isn't glaringly obvious to you how wrong you were.'

I blinked furiously, as the stinging turned to tears. 'I realise I could have been more... diplomatic.'

'*Diplomatic*? Jeez, Em. There was no need for it, full-stop. I would have helped Hetty pare down her story, and guided her from the beginning with her idea. We could have all helped. Instead, you humiliated her in front of everyone.'

'I – I didn't mean to. It was only what the others were thinking.'

'That gave you no right to say it. It was badly done, Em.' Jordi's words hammered into me like nails. Because he was right about this, at least.

I could take being chastised over Hetty. I'd let anger get the better of me, but then tried to justify it to myself, until I hadn't been able to see it for what it was.

Scalding tears fell freely now, and I rubbed them away with the back of my hand.

'I'll apologise to her,' I said, sniffling as the fight drained out of me, along with all my defensiveness and frustration.

I put down the phone to hunt for a tissue, half-expecting him to have rung off when I got back. But he hadn't. Of course not. That would never have been Jordi's style.

'Em, I'll be back soon. I *will*. We can't discuss everything over the phone like this. There's so much I still need to say...'

My agreement was muffled, subdued.

As we ended the call, I might have felt more reassured if he'd been able to look me in the eye.

Chapter 30

Polly was gracious enough to hear me out, without interrupting. We were on the sofa in my private sitting room – once the housekeeper's sanctuary and office, and redecorated a year ago with peony-pink wallpaper, and bright jewel-coloured cushions fringed with tassels perfect for fidgeting, which was what I was doing now, as Polly studied me over a large glass of wine.

I'd told her everything, explaining how she needed to hear this from me face to face. But when I finished, she didn't immediately launch into the rant I'd been steeling myself for. She merely carried on blinking at me, a dainty wrinkle between her brows.

'My head is seriously in a spin right now,' she admitted at last, sinking back against the cushions.

'You don't know how sorry I am. I've behaved abysmally.'

'How can you even say that word without lisping, Em?! Not that there's anything wrong with lisping. But is it some posh school thing; do they teach you how to say it? Anyway,' the wrinkle was more pronounced now, 'I'm mostly confused by why you're here – well, I know why *you're* here – but why Jordi isn't. And how come you're both acting like the sky has fallen in.'

This wasn't the response I'd expected. Polly oozed concern rather than indignation.

'Because... I went about it the wrong way. I should have told you how I was feeling before throwing myself at Jordi. I didn't know you'd decided you were only going to be friends—'

'You dipstick. You didn't know because you just won't listen to what I want. Or if you do, you won't accept it.' Polly shook her head vehemently, and reached for my glass, untouched on the coffee table. 'Here. Don't let me drink alone. You need to chill, girl.'

'And *you* don't need to talk like you're on reality TV.' But I took her advice and sipped at the wine. 'I do listen,' I said mulishly.

'Not nearly enough. This is all my fault too, though, because I'd had a hunch, an inkling, about your feelings for Jordi for ages. You couldn't seem to see it yourself, but the way you've always gone on about him, Em... I had to test it. And when I watched you together, I could tell you were both into each other. So I thought a prod from the green-eyed monster might stir you to action.'

'So you never fancied him? Not even a tiny bit?'

'Jordi is... fit, I'll admit – apologies for the rhyming – but he's not my type romantically. He's a hundred percent yours, though. It's a laugh being mates with him, and I've tried to help as much as I can when it comes to his work; the rest is up to him. But this anthology business, that's a *lot* my fault, too. For making the introductions. I didn't realise how much it would affect you.' She nudged me. 'See? I'm not perfect, either. So stop taking it out on your future husband and father of your babies. If you want them, that is. Babies.'

I took another gulp of wine. 'As if!'

Polly managed the biggest eye roll humanly possible. 'I give it a couple of years max till you're calling on my services as chief bridesmaid. I've always thought you should license this place as a wedding venue; the gardens would be a lush spot to tie the knot. It could be a good side hustle for you. Anyway, I also expect to be godmother to however many Midwynter McAndrew Daleys you might want to fill the Hall with, within reason. There's overpopulation and the planet to consider, plus those poonamis in the nappy ads.'

She gave a mock shudder. 'But perhaps think about consolidating your surnames better; though you're going to want to carry on the Midwynter lineage... Maybe Jordi can change *his* name?'

I was blushing profusely, though not from embarrassment, as such. It wasn't as if the idea of matrimony hadn't already – quite involuntarily – entered my head when it came to Jordi. Enough to make me swoon at the possibility. The forever-ness of it all. Even though I'd never been one of those people who lingered outside wedding emporiums, their entire big day playing out in front of them regardless of whether they'd met the person they wanted to make their vows to yet.

But Jordi and I had only just got together. And then somehow managed to pull abruptly apart. We weren't ready to contemplate a joint future if we couldn't get a handle on our relationship in the present.

There was so much more to think about besides how we felt. I couldn't make a lifetime commitment to anyone while I was like this, because when people came together, aspects of their lives naturally overlapped. I wanted to be able to support my partner in their world, too. And it would be irresponsible to consider bringing children into it while I couldn't even leave the Hall.

'Poll, stop.' I pinched her arm gently. 'You're missing the point of my confession.'

'I am?'

'You're supposed to be livid with me for moving in on Jordi behind your back. My actions could have made you unhappy. It goes against some sacred sisterhood.'

Polly frowned into her glass, running her finger around the rim. 'All joking aside then, is that why you're doing penance – or whatever this is? Pushing Jordi away? I think you've suffered all you need to, and I obviously can't forgive you quickly enough. You're going to do lasting damage, because you're making him suffer, too.'

'You're forgiving me?'

It couldn't be that easy, surely.

Her brow was a deep squiggle as she put down her glass, and before I knew it, she'd snatched mine out of my hands, too, and enveloped me in a tight embrace. 'Em, I was playing a dangerous game, hoping you'd wake up to how you felt by trying to make you jealous. It could have backfired. Actually, it seems like it did. To a degree.'

'It was a risky tactic, Poll,' I muttered into her hair, with a hollow, woeful note.

She sat back again, smiling regretfully. 'I know. But you and Jordi can fix it. I have faith in both of you.'

I managed a thin smile back, impatient to turn the subject on to her, wondering if she'd finally decided there was someone in her life she could feel that way about, too. When I'd written about this sort of thing in my books, women who were passionately in love themselves were usually the most lavish with their forgiveness.

'What about you and Zac, then? Have you taken it up a notch? You seemed to be getting on really well the other day.'

'Ha!' Polly scoffed. 'That's a whole other story right there.'

'What do you mean?'

'Well... if you'd been paying closer attention, you'd know Zac and I were direct with each other from the beginning. We were up for a bit of fun, but we weren't going to rush into anything, either. We've both been burned before.'

'Okay.' I tilted my head, trying to demonstrate I was listening.

'Well,' she said again, 'he was really keen on someone last summer. It was quite serious; they almost got engaged. One of the infant teachers at Pebblestow Primary, actually. But she got cold feet or something, and broke it off with him.'

'Sad.'

'I could tell he wasn't over Harriet completely. He got a faraway look in his eye whenever he brought her up. And then, a week or so ago, she got back in touch with him.'

I could sense where this was going. My heart flipped in

sympathy for my friend. 'So...?'

'They had a long conversation, and decided to give it another go. I know Harriet a bit from down the pub, and she *is* nice, I can't pretend she isn't. But I realise I'll have to fade out of the picture. Zac still wants to be mates, but it wasn't just platonic between us. There might have been a kiss and a cuddle here and there. That's all, though. Uncomplicated – which is what I wanted.'

She gave a hard shrug. 'I'd like him to have the best chance of making it work with her this time, Em. I don't need his friendship that badly I'm willing to jeopardise it all going wrong for him again.'

'You're being a good friend simply by stepping aside.' I pushed the glass back into her hand. 'I'm sorry. It sucks.'

'A bit,' she sighed, 'but not really. If it were me, I wouldn't want any sort of ex skulking that close to my boyfriend. Your dad and Randall get on freakishly well. I don't think I could do it.'

'Dad's a law unto himself. And it helps that Randall's got a worse golf handicap than him. See? I know that much. I couldn't have been zoned-out all the time.'

Polly chuckled.

I sighed. 'You're still going to help with the community garden, aren't you? I was counting on you.'

'I'm not missing out on the mayhem. And Mum's up

for it, too. But that's different from me and Zac hanging out on our own.' She squeezed my hand; seeing something in my face maybe that made her say, 'Listen, Em, don't think for one minute I regret meeting him. But I always knew Zac wasn't The One. Not mine, at least. I'm beginning to hope he exists, though. And that's a step forward – or backward, depending on viewpoint.'

I grinned jubilantly, unable to help myself. 'That's a new challenge for me right there. Who could possibly be worthy—'

'Don't you dare. Keep your dubious marriage-broking skills as far away from me as possible.' Polly snatched up the TV remote. 'Now, I think we need to forget about *lurve*' (she gave another mock shudder) 'for a couple of hours, and watch some gritty whodunnit – with a potty-mouthed female sleuth. We can try to work out who the murderer is. Closest wins... I don't know what. Prize to be decided. But Mum and I do this loads. I nearly always beat her.'

'You can stay over, if you want.' I swayed to my feet. 'Save getting your mum out late to pick you up.'

'I think I need my own car, which means pulling up my big girl pants,' she lamented. 'Or my own personal Uber, so I can still have a drink. Ooh, could I have the lilac room again, Em? With the chaise longue, and the wardrobe that looks like it might lead to Narnia?'

'It'll always be reserved for you, Poll. For as long as I'm mistress of Midwynter Hall. In fact, I'll put a name plaque on the door.'

'Yeah. Good. Don't turn that one into a nursery.'

I threw her a pouty glance.

And then I went to fetch more wine, and make buttery popcorn, and thank my lucky stars Polly Evans had rolled up at the Hall that afternoon two years ago, and that she'd brewed us a very strong pot of tea.

Chapter 31

Polly had done what Polly did best. She'd given me hope. A sunbeam to grab at among all the clouds.

'Please learn to communicate with Jordi better,' she'd implored, as we'd said our farewells after breakfast the next day. 'And the same goes for him with you. It'll make *all* our lives easier.'

So, that was my aim. Achievable, if I focused. Communicate better with a man I had somehow picked a quarrel with practically every time we'd ever talked.

Perhaps not so easy, when I put it like that.

But they hadn't always been full-blown disputes, very few of them in fact. More like... debates. And definitely not as upsetting as being berated over Hetty. That had stuck in my mind and lodged in my gut. I couldn't recall Jordi ever being as *disappointed* in me, not to my face, and it was far worse than grumpiness or exasperation or righteous anger.

I took special pains with my appearance on Saturday. It

might tip the balance in my favour if I was more desirable than he'd ever found me. Then again, this was Jordi we were talking about. We'd seen each other at our worst, or close enough. How I looked wouldn't be reason enough for him to stay or go. But still.

He messaged when he set off, and messaged again to say he was back at Donwell Cottage; but no invitation to go over, and I'd been too scared to be waiting for him this time when he arrived.

It was different now that he'd made himself at home there, though how long it was home remained to be seen. But for now, until he decided otherwise, it was his. I couldn't just let myself in whenever I wanted, even if I did have a key.

My dad came in from golf, and I fussed over him dutifully, announcing I'd made his favorite casserole.

'Jordi's back,' he said, almost as an afterthought as he headed off to get changed.

'Yes, I know,' I said, trying to be blithe about it, pretending to check on our supper in the Rayburn, while wondering how Dad knew.

'He turned up at the clubhouse.'

I jerked my head round. 'Oh?'

'Wanted to discuss becoming a member. I didn't realise he played as often as he did up in Lancashire. You never said, Emmeline.'

'I – I didn't know.' Or maybe Jordi had mentioned it, and I hadn't been listening. It was more than possible. So many failings, so little time.

But of paramount importance, Jordi wanted to join the golf club? That sounded... long-term.

Dad gave me a look I wasn't used to from him, as if he was seeing me as someone other than his faultless daughter. Furrows in his brow, and a slight downward hook to the lips. Something melancholy about it. Maybe resigned.

I stared back. 'What? What is it?'

'Nothing,' he muttered, and then turned to survey the kitchen, as if seeing that differently for the first time, too. 'The Hall's a big place, that's all; it would be eminently sensible if there were more than just two people occupying it one day. Though you've made it more than it ever was, Emmeline.'

'What do you mean?' I glanced around. 'It's just always been... home.'

'You made it *feel* like one.' My father hesitated, then strode over, pressing my hands between his. 'When I was growing up, it was nothing more than a draughty, shadowy old building. Just a shell, and a weight on my shoulders. I hate to admit it, and I never have before; not to you. You're right to look at me that way. But there was no charm, no wonder. I always felt the responsibility too heavily. No siblings, you see. My parents – good people though they were, God rest them – were counting on me to step up. I never planned that for you. I wanted to fill the Hall with laughter, not silence.'

'Dad.' I didn't know what to say.

'It wasn't to be. Your mother and I – we tried to be happy. But there was always something missing. We both love you, though, more than anything. No regrets.' He gazed around again. 'Anne began to breathe new life into the house, but you – you're the one who made it what it is today. You should be proud of that.'

'I just...' At a loss, I looked at the quarry-tiled floor. My father had never spoken so eloquently, or so persuasively. 'I love it, that's all.'

'I know. You made me realise how special it is. But we don't have to keep the whole estate to ourselves. We can do better. This commune thingy – it's a good place to begin.'

I didn't correct him this time. He knew what he was talking about.

'Anyway,' his hands slid from mine, 'I just thought it needed saying. I'm grateful, darling. And I don't want you to worry; I'm an adult, as your mother keeps reminding me. I shouldn't expect you to treat me like a child. I'm not incapable. I still have all my faculties. There are those less fortunate.'

His eyes clouded as he moved slowly towards the door. Was he thinking of Dean Daley? Of all the Daleys.

'Dad... I *like* looking after you. It's not a chore.'

'You need to look after yourself first, Emmeline. This place – it was never meant to be your cage. No one's saying you need to fly far, but you can't just flap your wings so enchantingly and never take off. It sounds lonely, not to be with your own kind.'

I could have said he was stretching the metaphor a little thin, but I was learning to filter my retorts more carefully.

I forced a nod.

'Oh.' He paused and turned again. 'Just one more thing...'

I wondered if he was trying to channel Columbo. It had been one of his favourite programmes to snooze through once, waking up every now and again with a mumble, to applaud the detective's mind games.

'What is it, Dad?'

'I nearly forgot.' Something told me he hadn't, but had simply timed it for maximum effect. With a self-congratulatory flourish, he plucked an envelope from his pocket. 'Jordi asked me to give you this.'

Chapter 32

I could only assume that asking me to meet him in the centre of the maze that evening was supposed to be symbolic. Something about losing our way and finding it again, probably.

Hopefully.

Jordi would delight in explaining, I was sure, especially if I didn't get it.

But, no. I was being too hard on myself, having possibly tipped too far the other way. And hard on him. Assuming lately that he was looking down on me from some lofty height, when for years he'd been trying to boost me up.

The days were at their longest. Even at this hour, there was more than enough light for me to hurry along the short, winding paths of neatly clipped hedges. I could picture the centre, with its curved stone bench, and Jordi waiting for me – not too impatiently, I hoped, as I'd changed my mind twice about what to wear and was now running late.

I felt butterfly-like in my most kaleidoscope of dresses, with its fluttery sleeves, smocked bodice and swirling skirt. My gold sandals were flat, ideal for the garden. Although I might have overdone it with the frou-frou rose clip in my hair, my bob less severe, as I hadn't had it trimmed in weeks.

Self-conscious suddenly, I took out the clip and stuffed it down my bra. A lack of pockets was a hazard.

As I rounded the last bend, heart pounding, hands clammy, relief zinged around inside me at the sight of Jordi, who'd clearly made an effort too, in smart dark shirt and trousers, leaping up from the bench when he spotted me.

It took a few moments for everything to sink in – the fairy lights just about visible in the shadows of the hedge, and the ice bucket and picnic basket. Even to my apparently clueless self, this didn't seem the sort of scene-setting where I was about to be told it had all been a huge mistake.

'Em,' he said, as I shivered to a halt a few feet away, 'you look... Wow.'

'Articulate as always, Jordi.' *Stop it, woman. Be nice.* 'You look very handsome, too,' I added, with a more civil tongue.

The longest pause. I waited, heart pounding harder as

if it might explode.

'So.' He faltered again. 'Us?'

And now my breath hitched at the fear in him, which had to be mirrored in me.

When I didn't answer quickly enough, he spoke again, stumbling over his words. 'I had the rollicking of my life when I told my mum what had happened. Before you ask, she got it out of me without resorting to torture. She said I should never have just left here like I did, or at least not without seeing you again, and I definitely shouldn't have sent that message saying we needed to thrash this out, like it was some kind of business deal—'

'Jordi.'

'Actually, wait, Em. *Please*? I'm on a roll here.' His eyes were too beseeching to overrule. 'I've been informed I worry about her too much, and I need to worry about myself more, and my own life for a change. She's got Matt, so she's not alone. I can have a break; she was adamant about that. And...' he took a deep juddery breath, 'apparently I haven't done nearly enough wooing.'

'Wooing? I echoed, my own breath just as juddery.

'This.' He gestured around the centre of the maze. 'You know. Romancing you.'

'Is that what this is?'

'If you want it to be. I'm just not good with the words.

I know that's bloody ironic. I tried writing it down – everything I wanted to tell you.'

'Freewriting?'

He groaned. 'I might have had a go.'

'As long as you don't re-read any of my books, looking for ideas, because I'll never need any of that stuff.'

'Good. My budget would never stretch to it. So, does this mean...?'

I realised I'd kept him hanging, though theoretically he hadn't asked a straightforward question. 'I still want this, Jordi.' My voice gained confidence. 'And I'm sorry if I ever made you doubt it. But you made me doubt it, too.'

I couldn't help getting that in. Was it raw honesty, or did I mean to sting a little? Always the nettle to his dock leaf.

Two steps on his part and I was caught up in his arms, lifted off the ground. He smelled divine; I wanted to just cling to him. But when I yelped, he virtually dropped me.

'What is it? Did I hurt you?'

'Not you.' I plunged my hand down my bra and fished out the hair clip. 'This.'

Jordi blinked. 'And it was down there because...?'

'I was wearing it, but I thought it was overkill, and I don't have pockets in this dress.'

He took it from me, examining the mechanism before

stepping close again and securing it in my hair. 'Not overkill. All I can see – all I ever see – is the stunning, obstinate, incredible Miss Midwynter.'

'Hmm.' I held on to his shirt to pull him closer. 'A bit less of the obstinate and a lot more of the incredible, please.'

His minty fresh tangled with mine, but when our kiss got too heated and our hands began to roam, we peeled ourselves away.

'We should sit, Jordi,' I said throatily. 'And talk. Remember?'

'Fizz?' He gestured to the bottle in the ice bucket.

'Glasses?'

'Shit.'

I tugged him down beside me on my new favourite bench. 'Drinking from the bottle is acceptable. But you have to pop the cork first.'

'Gee, really?'

Some things would never change. But sarcasm was beautiful when we did it our way. Within reason.

We passed the bottle back and forth, and dipped into the hamper to binge on ruby-red strawberries, and chocolate truffles dusted bronze and gold, which went impeccably with the champagne. And yet, we still couldn't speak the way I knew we had to.

The sky overhead darkened, bleached of colour. I rested my head on Jordi's shoulder, and conceded that perhaps there was time enough for talking. We seemed to be saying a lot without the need for words at all. Calm contentment and quiet companionship had much to offer. Sparring with my oldest friend was mentally stimulating, but maybe wiser in smaller doses from now on.

Eventually, though, after the bubbles from the champagne went up my nose for the second time, I animated myself.

'Jordi, I've just remembered something my dad said earlier. I didn't know you played golf so seriously. Enough to join a club, I mean.'

His grunt reverberated through both of us. 'I don't; I'll have to sneak in some practice. I just thought it was the best way of keeping your dad sweet. It's what your mum told Randall to do, when they first started going out – if my own mum can be believed.'

I laughed. 'You're joking?'

'I would never joke about our mothers,' he said soberly. 'Together, they're a thousand times better at matching people up than you'll ever be. That's what Mum reckons, anyway.' He coughed. 'Not that I approve, of course, about matchmaking in general.'

I sat up straight, to frown at him better. 'Jordi, you

didn't tell her *everything*, did you?'

'Not a blow-by-blow account, obviously.' He stopped, glancing at me. 'Am I as red as you, right now?'

'Very likely.' I rested my head hastily on his shoulder again. 'But she knows how I feel about you?'

'In their infinite wisdom, our mothers probably had us paired off over a decade ago.'

'Damn, they're good.'

'You know,' he said after another serene silence, as I hypothesised how half the champagne I'd consumed could have sunk to my feet while the other half had whooshed to my head, 'for someone who once wrote so epically about love and romance, you must have one hell of an imagination to get it so right. But you misapplied it radically in your own life. Not that I was much better.'

'Maybe we can be better together? I don't know if it's *easier* than being apart, but it sounds more entertaining; and "easy" wasn't making us all that happy.'

'Understatement.'

I sat up straight again, needing to get a piece of news off my chest. I'd hoped it might wait, not spoil the moment, but why did it have to? It was suddenly imperative he know.

'I rang a professional, Jordi. While you were gone. A therapist. Dr Perry Junior knows them; she gave me their contact details ages ago. They're supposed to be good.'

'Really?' His eyes drank me in. 'Wow.'

I was wowing him a lot, it seemed. A not unpleasant feeling.

'I haven't told anyone else yet. You're the first. And I can't make promises about what might happen...'

I wished I could.

I wished I could tell him I would be fine. That having someone who knew what they were doing, digging around in my brain alongside me, might uncover things I'd never understood about myself. Might free me forever. But I couldn't make guarantees like that. I had a suspicion it would be a gradual process, testing out strategies till we found one or two that worked. Or possibly something I could never shake off completely, clinging like a cobweb, even though I might learn to control it, enough to function Out There.

He gripped my hand. 'I'm beside you, Em. Whatever you need. One day at a time.'

'I'm doing this for me, Jordi. Not just us.'

'How it should be. You're the one who has to really want it. I can't want it for you; it isn't enough.'

'Thank you.' Head on shoulder again. This time I closed my eyes.

'It wasn't the only call you made, was it?'

I stirred again, looking at him.

'You spoke to Hetty...?'

'Oh.' Why couldn't the ground swallow me up? I took a swig of champagne instead, because the ground wasn't complying. 'I can't believe I was so rude.'

'You offered to mentor her, one-to-one? For as long as she needs?' Jordi seemed mystified; insultingly so. 'You realise that might be a very long time?'

'It could also end up being fun. Maybe I'll be a better teacher than you.'

'Do you think it might help your own writing?' he asked, tentative and low.

I wished I could tell him I'd be fine on that score, too.

But perhaps I had to grow up a little more. Or at least grow that thicker skin and not give a fig what happened beyond getting the words down.

When I didn't respond, Jordi said nimbly, 'Anyway, talking of teaching...'

'Crap. I'm awful.' I swivelled round to him on the bench. 'I didn't ask how it went with Mrs Goddard! Tell me she offered you a job on the spot.'

'No,' he chuckled, prising the bottle from my hands as if to imply I was hogging it. 'Nothing permanent. She's interested in my science skills, though. She wants to develop the STEM side of things more in the new school year. They haven't got anyone with my level of expertise, so I agreed they could pick my brains.' He heaved his shoulders. 'I don't know where it might lead, but it's as good a place as any to start.'

'They'll love you. They won't be able to live without you. I give it a term.'

'Really?'

'Make that half a term. Or even two weeks. Or just one assembly—'

He leaned close, and kissed me long and hard and flawlessly.

'Oh.' I pulled back, euphoric, and unable to resist one last taunt, which had nothing to do with my own perverse nature and was honestly the fault of the alcohol. 'I forgot something else.'

'What?'

'I had to carry on with the story, Jordi. While you were gone. Our story. I couldn't stop myself. And it's my best work yet. If it all comes true...'

'Em. No. Don't say that.'

I stood up, trying to sound cajoling as I snaked my arms around his neck, meeting little resistance. 'I'll let you read it.'

'I don't want to read it. I don't—'

My turn to kiss him, just as deeply and flawlessly, and

then I flopped into his lap, cackling. 'You fell too easily for that one, McAndrew Daley.'

He scowled, shaking his head. 'You don't deserve me.'

'I don't.' I grew serious, defying the giddiness from the champagne. 'But do you know why I really couldn't write it?'

'Why?' His arms pinned me tight against him, his eyes piercing yet forgiving.

I pressed a hand to his gorgeous, wonderfully familiar face, the pad of my thumb tenderly stroking his jaw.

All this 'wooing' had a lot to answer for.

'Because with you, Jordi, the magic will always be in *living* it.'

The End

Thank you!

I hope you enjoyed reading *Midsummer Magic at Midwynter Hall*. If you did, why not consider leaving a review, however brief, to help others find it, too. It would make a big difference to a little author. (I'm around five foot, so technically accurate.)

If you want to be first to hear all about my next book, and be in with a chance to win prizes in subscriber-only give-aways, consider signing up to my non-spammy newsletter. You can sign up directly from my website: lottiecardew.co.uk.

Or, if you haven't already read *A Christmas Wish on a Carousel* or *One Last Dream for December* they're both available now in eBook and paperback.

Another note from the author

For anyone interested in why I wrote this book...

You don't have to read this part. I mean, you can if you want, but it's not obligatory. Considering this was a shorter novel than my previous two, this additional note seems ironically long.

Anyway, if you've ever read *Emma* by Jane Austen, or watched the many films and TV adaptations, you might appreciate she isn't the most conventionally likeable of heroines. Austen herself apparently never expected her readers to side with her.

> 'I'm going to take a heroine whom no one but myself will much like.'
> [quote from Encyclopedia Britannica, and not just some vague, random source on the internet]

Yet Emma Woodhouse is one of her most enduringly brilliant and beloved characters. Definitely one of my favourites. Maybe because I was clueless once to some extent, too. Yes, there's a pun there, and if you know you know.

When I was twenty-one, I thought I could read people and understand what was going on between them, even if other things baffled me. I was deluded. I knew nothing. I was autistic, though I wouldn't know that either for another twenty-five years. As cracks in my knowledge became gaping holes, I started studying people to an almost scientific degree instead.

My version of Emma is likely neurodivergent herself, but she's only at the start of her journey to a possible diagnosis. My husband says I might not be capable of writing in first person viewpoint without that character coming out somewhere on the autistic/ADHD spectrum, whether they're aware of it or not. He means that in a good way, of course. I can *observe* neurotypical behaviour, but I don't know that I could *inhabit* an NT the way first person viewpoint demands.

(By the way, my husband's my rock, and my go-to with this book when I needed help with the golf terminology. And he won a comp at his club called the Jigger, before anyone writes in and says it isn't a thing.)

Emma., complete with full-stop, was the last film I watched in an actual cinema before the pandemic – which probably fixed it in my mind even more than it might have done otherwise. My daughter and I both loved it.

Lockdown came only days later, but I found I could 'do' quarantine rather well. Too well, as it turned out. Nowadays, you might see me on social media, happily gadding about without seeing the gaps in between, or without realising I've not really been out on my own since before the pandemic. Maybe once; twice at most. Very briefly. But that's it. There's often an unsettling amount of psyching myself up beforehand, even when I'm with other people and feel relatively safe.

Like so many conditions, though, agoraphobia is mis-understood, and affects people in different ways and to varying degrees. In short – although it's so much more complex – it's a fear and avoidance of places and situations where you might find yourself panicking or where you feel 'unsafe' and can't escape easily.

Over the last few years, I began to imagine what it might be like if I lived in a beautiful big house with acres of land I could roam around freely and everything I could possibly need delivered to my door. It would be even more of a struggle to venture into the 'scary' world beyond. And I realised it might be cathartic to write a story on that theme. Not a tale about healing, as such, because I don't know what that looks like. But about learning to ask for help. Em's 'recovery' in this book is just beginning. Though, who knows? It might not be anything like the path society would have us walk.

Jane Austen's Emma is also 'stuck'. Constrained by the village of Highbury and the small circle where she reigns as queen bee; trapped by the hierarchies she strictly adheres to, and the limitations of a woman in Regency England. Unlike Austen's other heroines, though, she's sitting on a small fortune and has no pressing need to marry. As heiress to Hartfield, her financial future and social status is assured. From a reader's point of view, does she have to work harder to elicit our sympathy?

Perhaps as the 2020 movie was so imprinted on me, with its slight spicing up of the central love story and the way it made the age difference more palatable to modern audiences – especially young women like my daughter – and having always wanted to write a book inspired by Austen's plot, I soon realised I could link the two ideas. My own Em needed to be a rich but restricted heiress, too, and to help feed her delusions about her matchmaking abilities, I made her an agoraphobic romantic novelist.

Anyway. I loved dropping in all the references to the original material, and I hope you enjoyed spotting them.

This was never meant to be a faithful retelling, a modernised version of *Emma*. It was simply inspired by Jane Austen's flawless novel about a young woman coming to terms with her flaws. A pleasure – and perhaps a relief – to write, though not actually the book I'd set out to work on next in the Pebblestow universe. For personal reasons, I had to take a break from that one.

Yet, weirdly, things started to happen in my life while I wrote *Midsummer Magic at Midwynter Hall* that had me wondering if maybe I have some freaky ability to pen the future myself, but I won't bore you with that. Let's call it coincidence and move on. I need to wind things up here.

So, huge gratitude if you've read this far; I hope you enjoyed my latest offering. With thanks, too, to all the remarkable people who make my writing life possible – my lovely husband, my incredible children, my fabulous parents and extended family, my amazing friends who put up with me, and the wonderful readers who reach out and make it so worthwhile. You all deserve those glowing adjectives and more.

Love Lottie xx

A Christmas Wish on a Carousel

When Cara Mia Shaw makes a desperate wish one night, while riding on a carousel at a Christmas market, little does she know her small, but safe world is about to spin off its axis.

Befriending a fascinating elderly woman called Perdita might set Cara on a different, albeit harder, course in life – if she's brave enough to listen. And then there's the new man she's dating, and the other one who comes along just to complicate matters. But will she self-sabotage as usual or gamble everything this time, including her heart?

It might take the highs and lows of friendship, the risk of a forbidden romance, and a Pomeranian called Loki – not to mention some much-needed festive magic – before Cara finally realises the wish she made that night on the carousel might just be about to come true...

One Last Dream for December

· ❤ · ❤ · ❤ · ❤ · ❤ ·

Esme Blythe has led a nomadic existence for years, never thinking she fits anywhere, and never feeling she's earned the right to. But when she moves in above Percival's, a charming old toy shop, it seems the village of Pebblestow is about to weave its signature fairy-tale magic.

Surrounded by wooden soldiers, rocking horses, and vintage doll's houses, not to mention the locals who seem determined to be part of her life, Esme has to face up to everything she's been missing, or turn her back on an incredible opportunity.

New friends, formidable foes, and the thrill of a budding romance, conspire to make this the most bittersweet December ever. But when she finally learns the truth about the toy shop's owner, her elusive benefactor, the mysterious Mr Percival, is it already too late for Esme to change her mind... and heal her heart?

About the author

Lottie Cardew writes witty(ish), heartstring-tugging rom-coms with little flourishes of magic. She lives in North Wales, UK, subdues the other members of Novelistas Ink if they misbehave – including the popular authors Trisha Ashley and Sophie Claire – and is an advocate for neurodiversity in fiction. Lottie is diagnosed autistic with suspected ADHD. Her home is overrun by husband, not-very-small children (in fact, they're technically adults), and a ball of fluff masquerading as a Pomeranian, so Lottie frequently takes refuge at her desk.

lottiecardew.co.uk
Twitter / X: @MsLottieCardew
Facebook: LottieCardew – Author
Instagram: @bossynovelista

Printed in Great Britain
by Amazon